# The Settlement
# Ali Spooner

# The Settlement

## Ali Spooner

Affinity
eBook Press
NZ
2015

The Settlement

© Ali Spooner 2015

Affinity E-Book Press NZ LTD
Canterbury, New Zealand

1st Edition

ISBN: 978-0-908351-00-8

Editor: Ruth Stanley
Proof Editor: Alexis Smith
Cover Design: Irish Dragon Designs

# Acknowledgments

I would like to thank JC for sharing her hometown and the Annual Dove Hunt with me. I hope you will enjoy the creative license I took with establishing some of the characters in town. That weekend was very memorable for me and I had to share the wonderful experience of a Women Only Dove Hunt. Witnessing the relationships developed across many generations of women was heartwarming, and I look forward to participating again soon.

## Dedication

To Lexie, I hope you remember how much we love you. Leann Womack said it best, "When you get the chance to sit it out or dance, 'I Hope You Dance.'"

# Table of Contents

**Also by Ali Spooner**

Terminal Event
Love's Playlist
Cowgirl Up
Twisted Lives
The Epitaph
Bailey's Run
Sugarland
Bayou Justice

# Chapter One

The sun kissed her face as Cadin Michaels carefully maneuvered her Harley Davidson down a winding country road. The wind wrapped around her, lifting her dark hair and her spirits as she rode away from her tortured past toward an unknown future.

The night before, in her Atlanta penthouse, she spread a map of the Southeast across her home office wall. She picked up a dart and hurled it at the map without aiming, and then walked forward to see where it had landed.

"Greensboro, Alabama," she said. "Greensboro it is then."

Cadin left the office and walked to the large bedroom she had shared with her partner Missy Dupree until six months ago. She opened an expansive closet, took out six pairs of Levi's and a dozen shirts and placed them on the king-sized bed in the center of the room. Back to the closet where in the far back corner a dark green duffel bag, one issued by the US Army, sat waiting for the trip. The name Michaels had been stamped on the material in black ink. The ink had faded, but the material was in excellent shape. The bag had belonged to David, her older brother and a helicopter pilot shot down during the Desert Storm operations, leaving her an only child. A soldier had delivered his personal effects to her family in the bag and Cadin had kept it in his memory.

Cadin worshipped her big brother and only sibling. His death had sent her spiraling into a deep depression, one she could not wake from until Missy appeared in her life, rescuing her from the funk of her misery.

Missy, a social worker, had come to her office one day to request a donation for a local women's charity she worked for, and Cadin had fallen for her instantly. Her shiny blond hair and emerald eyes mesmerized Cadin from the start. She had listened to Missy's request with an open mind and could sense the passion the woman had for this cause. Missy left her office that day with a large donation and a piece of Cadin's heart.

✝

Six months earlier…

"God forgive me," Cadin groaned as she watched the nurse reach up to the bank of machines next to Missy's bed. The nurse turned to look at the small group gathered in the room and one by one they nodded. She watched as the nurse's fingers trembled slightly as they landed on the button that fed power to the ventilator that breathed life into Missy's body. Her heart pounded in her ears as she stood beside the hospital bed and gazed down at her lover. Missy's pale body was cold to the touch. There was no machine invented that could bring the warmth of life back to her body. The doctors had pronounced her 'brain dead' three days earlier, with no hope of ever regaining consciousness. The machines pumped breath into her body and forced her heart to keep beating, but she knew Missy would never want to go on like this.

Cadin looked up at the woman standing at the opposite side of the bed and her heart wrenched with pain. Marilyn, Missy's twin sister, stood staring down at her sister. When her tear-filled eyes looked up at Cadin, she nodded slowly.

"We both know she wouldn't want to be kept like this," she said.

"I know, but I just don't think I can watch," Cadin cried.

"We can do this together," a soft voice spoke from the end of the bed.

Cadin had forgotten her mother was in the room. Marcel reached for Marilyn's hand and together they walked to stand beside her. "Together," Marcel said.

Cadin nodded and slipped her hand inside Missy's as the nurse pressed the button.

Alarms immediately sounded in the room and the nurse rushed to turn them off with the exception of the heart monitor, then left them in peace.

They turned back to face the bed as the nurse left the room. Cadin's eyes searched the heart monitor to see the rate dropping quickly. "I will always love you, my darling," she whispered and leaned down to kiss Missy's lips one last time.

She held her hand as her heart rate plummeted, and when the last beat came whispered, "Goodbye, my love."

When no other beat followed, Marcel led Marilyn from the room and waited outside for Cadin.

Tears flowed down her cheeks at the look of relief on Missy's face. "I will make them pay for this, if it's the last thing I do," she vowed as her grief burned with rage.

† 

Three days after the funeral Marcel finally consented to going back to her condo in Florida. Marilyn would fly home the next day. She rode with Cadin to drop her mother at the airport.

"Thank you for being here," Marilyn said. "Missy loved you like a mother."

"She was my second daughter," Marcel said. "I was honored to know her even if it was a short time."

"She will always be in our hearts," Marilyn assured her.

"Are you sure you don't want me to go in with you?" Cadin said as they pulled up to the curb outside of ticketing.

"No, I'm good. I can manage from here. I'll call you tonight to let you know I've made it home."

Cadin walked to the trunk to remove her mother's bag. "Are you sure I can't stay longer?" Marcel asked.

"I appreciate you so much, Mom, but I need to be on my own right now," Cadin said.

"I'm only a phone call away," Marcel said as she hugged her daughter.

Cadin managed a weak smile. "I love you, Mom."

"I love you too. You could always fly down for some beach time you know."

"Thanks Mom. I'll wait for your call tonight."

Marcel hugged Marilyn and picked up her bag. "Take care of you," she said and walked inside the terminal.

✝

Cadin picked over the salad they had prepared for dinner. "Do you plan to go back to work soon or take some time off?" Marilyn asked.

"I think I'll go back next week, but there's something I need to do first. I wanted to discuss it with you before taking any action."

"What is it?"

"I plan on suing the hospital over Missy's death, and I plan to start a foundation in her honor."

"Do you really think she would want that?" Marilyn asked.

"They have to be made to pay for ruining her life. She did so much good work for the community. There has to be a way to continue her legacy. I know she would agree to that."

"Do you have any idea what the foundation would support? Scholarships, or something like that?"

"That part hasn't come to me yet," she admitted. "I have to win the suit for her first."

"You know I'll support whatever you decide. It won't bring her back, but it would carry on the work she loved."

"I have to do this for her," Cadin said with tears in her eyes. Even looking at Marilyn pained her. Marilyn's hair was a shade darker and curlier than Missy's, but they had the same green eyes. Her heart ached for the loss of her lover, and though she loved Marilyn and appreciated her being here for support, looking at her twin reminded her so much of Missy.

Marilyn moved around to take Cadin in her arms. "I know you do, and you'll come up with something really great."

They talked deep into the night and when they went to bed, Cadin cried herself to sleep snuggled into Missy's pillow.

†

After dropping Marilyn at the airport the next morning, she stopped by her office. Her business partner, Pam Jordan, met her at the door to her office.

"It's good to see you. How are you feeling?"

"Lost and still in shock, I think."

"I think that's a pretty normal response. It's only been a few days. So what are you doing here? I didn't expect you back before next week."

"I want you to do something for me."

"What can I do?"

"I want you to set up a foundation for me. I plan to sue the pants off the hospital and the physician that killed Missy, and I want to use the settlement to establish a foundation in her honor to continue the work she loved."

"I can do that," Pam said. "Have you filed suit yet?"

"I've finished the draft. I'm going to review it today and send it to the hospital attorney later. If he's smart he'll approach me with a mediation request quickly."

"Are you sure that's what you want to do?"

"I made a promise to Missy to make them pay for what they did to her. I know it won't bring her back, but they need to pay." Cadin looked at her friend. They had been law partners for ten years. "I'm not asking you to participate; just set up the foundation and sit on the board with Marilyn and me."

"I will do whatever you need me to do, but I'm worried about you. If you're involved in a suit, you won't be able to grieve properly. Can't we engage another firm to handle it for you?"

"There's no way I'll give up forty percent to a firm on such a slam-dunk case. I handle wrongful death cases all the time remember?"

"But not one regarding your lover," Pam argued.

"I know it's crazy, but no one will handle the case with the passion I can bring to it."

"I definitely can't argue with that," Pam said and wrapped her arms around her partner.

Cadin smiled for the first time since entering the office. "The crazy part or the passion?" she teased.

"Both. I'll start drafting the papers this week," she said. "Now get out of here before I put you to work."

"Thanks Pam. I'll see you Monday."

"Call if you need anything."

"I will," Cadin said and left the office.

†

Cadin rode the elevator up to the penthouse and sighed deeply as she unlocked the door. This was the first time she had been alone in the apartment since Missy's death and the dread weighed heavy on her shoulders. She stepped through the door and turned to hang her keys on the key holder one of Missy's clients had made for her. The keys to Missy's SUV hung where she had left them, the day she went to the hospital for what was supposed to be a simple procedure.

She walked over to the sofa and collapsed into the soft cushions. The silence closed in around her. Cadin imagined closing her eyes and hearing Missy's cheerful banter echoing through the rooms.

✝

Missy had invited Cadin to a fund-raising event a week after their first meeting and afterward invited her for a drink. They talked and laughed late into the night and it wasn't long before they realized there was more than a friendship growing between them. It had been six years since Missy had walked into her life and now she was gone, never to return.

Missy had suffered with gallstones and the surgeon she had met with assured her that it was a simple procedure and that he performed on average five surgeries per day, many the same procedure she would be having. Scheduled to be his third procedure of the day, Cadin waited anxiously beside Missy. Surgery would last less than two hours and she would spend a night in the hospital before going home. His second case of the day had developed complications during the procedure and instead of postponing her case he kept on schedule without taking a break between surgeries.

Maybe it was exhaustion or just a general lack of focus, but during Missy's procedure he severed a major artery, triggering cardiac arrest as her body bled out. The team worked feverishly to save her life, but the loss of blood and oxygen to her brain could not prevent damage to her brain. Tests revealed she had total loss of brain function. There was no hope of recovery. The only decision left was when to pull the plug on the machines.

At first Cadin argued that Missy should be given time to see if she would make a recovery, but common sense and the pleading of her twin sister to let her go convinced Cadin it was the right thing to do.

Cadin fell asleep with the sound of a dying heartbeat ringing in her ears.

When she woke three hours later curled up on the sofa, reality closed around her heart with a steel grip. Missy was gone, and she was all alone. She stood and walked to the bar to pour the first of many drinks she would consume that night and then powered up her computer.

She finalized the draft of her suit, emailed it to the respective counsel for the hospital and the physician of the anesthesiology group, filing for wrongful death, medical negligence, and malpractice. When she pushed the button to send the email she stood and rushed to the bathroom to purge her body of the whiskey poisoning her memories. Cadin showered and then crashed naked onto her bed.

† 

Within a week, Cadin had begun dialoguing with the opposing counsel and had a date set for mediation a month away.

She managed to struggle through her work, delving into her cases to delay returning home to an empty apartment.

The first mediation ended without a settlement and Cadin told them to prepare to go to trial as she exited the office. She was furious at their pitiful attempts to settle the case at a pittance of what it was worth. Cadin's resolve steeled and she was determined to play hardball as the price of her settlement award skyrocketed.

Two weeks later, she received a request for a second mediation attempt. The attorneys had begun the discovery process and realized the indefensible case they were faced with and reconsidered reaching a settlement.

Six months after Missy's death, Cadin received an award check for ten million dollars, and a signed agreement that the physician would make a personal donation of one hundred thousand dollars each year to Missy's Foundation on the date of her death for the next ten years. From her years of practice, Cadin understood the insurance carrier would make the settlement payment, and she wanted to ensure the man would not forget the fatal error he made that cost Missy her life. She felt little satisfaction with the award, and without the battle for the settlement to focus on, Cadin felt more lost than ever.

When she returned to the office the following Monday morning, she handed Pam the check.

"Holy shit, you did it," Pam said.

Cadin sat on her office sofa and looked at her with a blank expression.

"What's wrong?"

"Missy was my life and I'm so lost without her. I don't know how I go about finding me again."

Pam walked over to sit beside her. "I think, my friend, it's time for you to take a sabbatical and find who you are and make some decisions about how you will administer Missy's Foundation."

"But how, I have no clue," Cadin admitted.

"Pull out that Fat Boy you used to love to ride and hit the road. Just ride and think. See some places you've never been."

Cadin allowed the suggestions to sink in and she thought Pam was onto a great idea. "You know, you're right. Is this the right time to leave you on your own though?"

"Business is steady, but nothing I can't handle for a few months. Go find the Cadin I love again. Quite honestly the new you is bumming me out," Pam teased.

"Let me finish up a few projects and I'll take off next week."

"That sounds like a plan. Let's go deposit this check and I'll buy you an early lunch," Pam said.

# Chapter Two

Cadin rode hard all morning until she reached Greensboro then pulled into a gas station to fuel the bike. She looked across the small town square and found something mysteriously missing. There was no sign of a hotel, bed-and-breakfast, or boarding room in sight. Going inside to pay for her fuel she smiled at the middle-aged woman behind the counter.

"Can you tell me if there's a hotel nearby?"

"Not unless you consider 'nearby' as fifty miles. There's a flop-and-drop frequented by truckers twenty miles away at the main highway, but I wouldn't recommend it. It's one of those places you leave with more than you came with, if you catch my drift," she said with a knowing smile.

Cadin wasn't exactly sure she "caught her drift," but she did know she didn't want to find out for certain what the woman meant. She felt like her decision to come to Greensboro was becoming a bad one, but decided to ask one more question.

"So what do you do for local accommodations?"

"Well, we don't get many visitors, and most stay with family or friends."

Cadin felt her hope slipping away, and her face formed a frown.

"However, Sister Frances runs the local women's shelter, and would gladly offer you accommodations for a short period."

"That would be perfect," she said, her smile returning. "Can you give me directions?"

Cadin paid for her fuel and then returned to her bike for the short ride. She pulled into the drive of the address the clerk had given her just as the sun was fading. She walked up to the front door of the white clapboard home and rang the bell.

Cadin heard footsteps from inside the house while she waited for the door to open. She was surprised when the heavy door swung open and a slight girl of six or seven opened the door. Her light brown curls fell to her shoulders and her green eyes grew wide as she looked up at Cadin.

"Are you Sister Frances?" she asked to tease the young girl.

The child grinned, revealing a dimple in her left cheek.

The action reminded her of Missy, how her green eyes sparkled when she smiled. Her heart soared with the memory of her lover, but plummeted when the reality returned and Cadin remembered she would never look into those eyes again.

The girl giggled. "No, I'm Lexie," she said.

"Is Sister Frances around?"

"Yes, ma'am, she's in the kitchen with Mama," she said without moving away.

"Do you think I could talk to her?"

The small child surprised her by reaching up and taking her hand. "Come with me and I'll take you to her," she said as she pulled Cadin deeper into the house. She couldn't help but grin as she followed Lexie to the large kitchen.

When they stepped into the room, her eyes fell on three women talking behind the counter. One woman was an adult-sized version of Lexie, who she assumed was the child's mother. Cadin stood motionless, riveted by the deep green eyes that peered back at her until the banging of a pot broke her concentration.

"May I help you?" a heavyset older woman asked.

"I hope so. I'm looking for Sister Frances. Bev at the gas station told me she could offer me accommodations for a few days, and I can pay," she added for good measure.

"I'm Sister Frances," she said and stepped forward to offer her hand.

"Cadin Michaels," she said as she clasped the warm hand, rough from long hours of labor, and shook it firmly. "I'm going to be in town for a few days and I didn't realize there wasn't a hotel until I got here."

"Never has been. We had a boarding house back in the sixties, but it didn't last long." She looked at Cadin with curiosity. "What brings you to town? Not many from out of town visit these days."

Cadin thought of an answer for several seconds. "Fate," she finally answered.

"Well, that's quite a large answer, but I don't have time to pursue it right now. We've got to finish dinner." She looked down at Lexie. "Will you be a good girl and take Cadin to the sleeping quarters and show her around for me?"

"Yes, ma'am," Lexie said, wearing a proud smile.

"We eat promptly at six," Sister Frances said.

"Is there anything I can help with?"

"Not tonight, but thank you. Take the time to get settled in and familiar with the grounds."

"May I pull my bike around back?"

"Yes, there's a small covering, you may park beneath."

"I'll meet you out back then," she said to Lexie and turned to step away then stopped. "Do I need to pay in advance?"

"No, we'll discuss that later," Sister Frances said and went back to rolling out biscuits.

Cadin nodded and turned to walk back out the front door to her bike. She started the motor and drove slowly around the house to the covered area Sister Frances had spoken of and parked her bike.

Lexie ran up to her as she stepped off her bike. "Can I carry anything for you?"

"Sure, you can carry this for me," she said and handed Lexie her helmet.

Lexie took the helmet as Cadin busied herself releasing the duffel from the back of her bike.

"That's all you have?" Lexie asked innocently.

"Yeah, it is," she answered with a grin. "It's hard to carry much more on a motorcycle."

Lexie led her inside a long building that looked like a dormitory or bunkhouse. Row after row of twin bunk beds filled the room. There were four other women and two small children in the room, and they smiled as she and Lexie entered.

"You can have any of these beds," Lexie said, pointing to a row of beds.

"Which one is yours?

"This one. Mama sleeps on the bottom and I'm up top."

Cadin took her helmet and placed it beneath the foot of the bed next to the ones Lexie had pointed out. There were several empty clothes hangers dangling from the base of the top bed, so she pulled her jeans and shirts out of the bag to hang them at the foot of the bed. The rest of the clothing she left in her bag and pushed it beneath the twin bed.

"Do you want me to show you around?"

"That would be great."

Lexie took her by the hand again and led her across the long room to a door. "This is the bathroom and shower area," she explained.

Six shower stalls, six enclosed toilets, and four sinks lined the wall. A large shelf held clean towels, washcloths, and bed linens. The sparsely decorated area smelled fresh and clean. Lexie allowed her to take in the room and then led her outside.

"This is our play area," she said.

She stepped into an ancient pecan orchard with large trees, spaced precisely with level plots between them. There were several swings and other toys visible along with several bicycles. Cadin felt an item rolling beneath her boot. She bent down to pick up a fully matured pecan.

"Sister Frances pays me a penny apiece for every pecan I harvest for her," Lexie said.

"That sounds like a good deal," Cadin said. She checked the time to find that it was quickly approaching six. "We better head to the dining room. I would hate to miss out on dinner."

"Tonight is pot roast, veggies, and biscuits," she said. "One of my favorites."

"How long have you been here?"

"Since we left home," Lexie said, unaware of the time frame.

Cadin smiled at the child's innocence and opened the door to the back of the house revealing a large room filled with picnic tables and benches. Two of the tables were set with plates, cups, and utensils.

Sister Frances and two women began bringing out dishes from the kitchen, pitchers of tea, and several gallons of milk.

"May I help carry anything?" she asked.

"You and Lexie can bring the biscuits," Sister Frances said with a warm smile.

Sister Frances was slicing the roast when they returned. "You can place the biscuits in the middle of the table and take your seats."

Cadin put the platter on the table and then took the seat Lexie was pointing to. Once they were seated, Sister Frances took the hands of the women seated on either side of her and bowed her head. The rest of the people around the table also joined hands as Sister Frances said a short prayer.

"Amen," Lexie said after the prayer ended.

"Would you care to introduce yourself to the group, Cadin?" Sister Frances asked.

"Well, my name is Cadin Michaels and I'm from Atlanta. I recently lost someone very dear to me, so I've decided to take some time away from work to find out who I am."

"Welcome, and I'm sorry for your loss," the adult-sized Lexie said. "My name is Terri Foster, and you have already met my daughter Lexie."

"Yes, I have, and might I say she's a wonderful tour guide."

"My name is Betty Duncan, and like you I have lost someone close to me," said an older woman sitting on the other side of Sister Frances. "My husband of forty-five years. Henry passed away suddenly six months ago."

"I'm sorry to hear that. Forty-five years is impressive," Cadin said.

"We were sweethearts from elementary school," Betty said.

The other women introduced themselves and their children, but did not elaborate on the circumstances that brought them to Sister Frances. With the introductions complete, the group began eating the wonderful meal.

"I can see why this is one of your favorite meals, Lexie," Cadin said. "This food is terrific."

"Eat all that you want," Sister Frances said.

"Thanks," she said and selected another biscuit.

After everyone had finished eating, they all pitched in to clean up the kitchen, store leftovers, and wash the dishes. Cadin volunteered to wash and Lexie eagerly requested to dry the dishes, with her mother's help of course.

When everyone else had left the kitchen, except for Terri, Lexie and Cadin, Sister Frances asked them if they would like some hot cocoa.

"That would be great," Lexie answered.

"I suppose you'll want marshmallows too?" Sister Frances asked.

"Yes, please, if you have some."

"How can you have hot cocoa without them?"

"Not very well," Lexie answered.

"Well, let's get to it," Sister Frances said.

Cadin and Terri returned to sit at the picnic table.
"You have a great daughter."

"Thanks, Lexie has definitely been the highlight of
my life," Terri answered.

"How long have you been here?"

"Almost three weeks. Her dad got sentenced to ten
years in state prison, so we took advantage of an opportunity
to leave and get a fresh start."

"Is Lexie close to her dad?"

"Quite the opposite, she's terrified of him. He's not a
nice man, especially when he's been drinking, which was
almost constantly. We aren't married, so I have no qualms
over leaving him in jail."

"Even if you were married, I think it's still a good
decision for the two of you. What are your plans for the
future?"

"We like it here and I've got a job at the grocery
store. Sister Frances will allow us to stay until I can save
enough to start out on our own."

"That's very generous of her," Cadin said.

"She's been great to us since we arrived, our car
floating in on fumes and my wallet empty."

Cadin looked across the room to watch as Sister
Frances placed Lexie on the counter and they chatted while
they made the hot cocoa. She smiled brightly as Lexie told
her a story, her body animated as she shared her tale.

"What about you? What are your plans?" Terri asked.

"To settle here for a few days and then do some more
traveling," Cadin said. "Eventually I'll make my way back to
Atlanta."

"What do you do there?"

"I'm a lawyer," she answered.

"Wow," Terri said impressed.

"Even lawyers have screwed-up lives at times," Cadin said. "Mine is definitely screwed up."

"I'm very sorry. Do you mind me asking what happened?"

Cadin hesitated for a second, sharing such personal information. *What the hell, she's a complete stranger and after a few days I'll never see the woman again.* "Missy, my lover and partner of six years, went into the hospital for a simple surgical procedure. Things went terribly wrong and she died."

"Oh my goodness, I'm so sorry," Terri said.

"Thanks," Cadin said and looked up to find Sister Frances and Lexie had entered the dining area. She didn't know how much she had heard, but then it didn't really matter. She was surprised she was able to tell a stranger about Missy, without breaking into tears or flying into a rage.

✝

"Here we go, ladies, hot cocoa with marshmallows," Sister Frances said as she placed a tray on the table holding the four mugs.

The group drank their cocoa and Terri announced, "I think it's time for showers and bed for us, young lady."

"Okay, Mommy," Lexie said. Cadin could hear the sleepiness in her voice. "Will you still be here tomorrow Cadin?"

"Yes, I will see you in the morning."

"Goodnight then," she said and hugged Cadin.

She and Sister Frances watched them leave the kitchen. "Lexie sure seems taken with you," she said as Cadin carried empty mugs to the sink and washed them.

"For some weird reason kids seem to be attracted to me," Cadin said with a shrug.

"That's not a bad thing," Sister Frances said.

"No, I guess it's not," Cadin said as she reached into her pocket and pulled out a fifty-dollar bill. She handed it to her host. "Will this cover the first night?"

"That will cover two nights. I usually don't charge paying guests but twenty-five dollars a night."

"I would have had to pay four times that amount for a hotel," Cadin said. "One night," she repeated.

"Thank you," Sister Frances said as she tucked the bill into her pocket.

"So, how does a newcomer get in on this pecan harvesting enterprise?" she asked with a grin.

"I hate to inform you, but you are too old," she said with a chuckle. "I offer that opportunity only for children under ten to give them a goal to work for and an opportunity to make a few dollars. It's also a good way to keep them constructively occupied while their mothers find work in town."

"That's a great idea. What do you do with the nuts?"

"We have a small farmers market twice a month on Saturdays, and I sell them there. I crack and shell some, others I sell whole," she explained. "I don't know if it's all this global warming stuff or what, but the nuts have dropped a good month early this year."

"I can't really say much about global warming, but it was a mild winter and an early spring, so maybe Mother Nature's clock is just a bit off," Cadin offered.

"I reckon, but I'm not complaining," Sister Frances added with a smile.

"Would you mind if I help Lexie out a bit? I could use some fresh air."

"That would be fine. The nuts are dropping like crazy and I need to get them off the ground soon. I can pay you, but not as much as it's worth."

"Nonsense, pay our little nut harvester your agreed upon price."

"Lexie's a good kid and Terri did the right thing to leave when she could," Sister Frances said.

"May I ask another question?"

"Sure."

"Why is Miss Betty here?"

"That's a sad story. Her husband had been very ill, but kept it secret from her. His illness and the mounting medical bills caused him to fall behind on their mortgage payments and when he died suddenly, the bank foreclosed on her for a little over twenty thousand dollars."

Cadin shook her head in disbelief. "They wouldn't work with her on payments?"

"No, and to make matters worse, she's eligible to draw social security benefits on her husband's record, but after she applied, the caseworker quit and her application disappeared, so she had to start the process over." Sister Frances shook her head. "Hopefully she will start receiving benefits in the next month or so and can find a place to rent. I've told her she can stay here as long as she wants, but she's a proud woman. She's a great deal of help to me here."

"Do you know what bank foreclosed on her?"

Sister Frances chuckled. "The only one we have in town."

"Could you give me the address on Miss Betty's home?"

"Sure I can, but what are you up to?"

"Just a little investigation," Cadin said.

"I'll write it down for you after breakfast if that's okay. I'm bushed and think I'll head off to bed."

"That would be perfect and thank you for allowing me to stay."

"You are more than welcome," Sister Frances said and walked across the room. "Turn the lights out when you're done please."

"I'm headed to bed soon too," Cadin said and flipped the light switch as she went out the back door.

✝

She walked over to a small bench near the pecan orchard and looked up at the cloudless night sky. Cadin could not remember ever seeing the stars as clearly as she did right now. The lack of artificial light made the sky glitter with the brilliant stars and the full moon was huge in the clear sky. A cool breeze had picked up while she was inside and she felt goose flesh rise on her arm. She stood and stretched before returning to the sleeping quarters as quietly as she could.

✝

Lexie was sleeping soundly when Cadin entered the room. Terri was sitting on the bed folding a basket of clean clothes. A pair of freshly pressed jeans and a uniform top for the local grocery were hanging at the end of the bed.

"Do you have to work tomorrow?"

Terri looked up at her. "Yes, I go in at seven and work until three."

23

Ali Spooner

"Would you mind if I helped Lexie harvest some pecans tomorrow after running a few errands?"

"She would love that. Miss Betty watches over her for me when I work, but I'm sure she wouldn't mind a break."

"Okay, so next question. If she asks, may I take her for a ride on my bike?"

Terri hesitated for a few seconds. "Do you have a second helmet?"

"Yes, but it will probably be huge on her. I promise I will be extremely careful."

"I'm sure you would, so yes, when she asks, it's okay with me."

"Thank you. You have one fine little woman there," Cadin said.

"I know. She's six going on sixteen somedays."

"Will she be starting school soon?"

"She will be in first grade in three weeks. She's so excited to meet new kids and make friends."

"I bet she is," Cadin said as she took out shorts, a T-shirt, and her hygiene bag. "I think I'll hit the shower and get some sleep."

"Goodnight then, Cadin. If I don't see you in the morning, have a good day."

"Thanks, you too," she said and left the room.

She showered and prepared for bed. When she returned to the sleeping room, Miss Betty was the only one still awake. She sat up in her bed reading, a small lamp giving her light. She looked up and smiled at Cadin.

"Goodnight," Cadin whispered.

†

The fresh country air and the long ride took a toll on Cadin who slept soundly through the night. The next morning she smiled and fought back laughter when a rooster woke her with his crowing. She climbed from the bed and dressed. She made the bed quietly and then walked outside.

The morning was dawning brilliantly. The cool air felt good on her skin. She looked toward the main house and found that lights were on in the kitchen. Terri and Miss Betty were sitting at a picnic table drinking coffee. Terri was finishing a light breakfast of eggs and toast.

"May I fix you some breakfast?" Miss Betty asked.

"I can fix it," Cadin said.

"Nonsense, besides I love cooking," she said. "Grab a cup of coffee and keep Terri company until she has to leave for work."

Cadin chuckled and went to the counter to fix a cup of coffee. She had a growing suspicion that arguing with Miss Betty would prove fruitless, so she conceded and allowed her to prepare her breakfast.

"You are up early," Terri said as Cadin sat across from her.

"I slept well last night and I'm usually an early riser. I did have to chuckle when that rooster started crowing."

"That's Roscoe. He's the neighbor's pride and joy, but sometimes he gets his times a little confused," Terri said.

"I can't say as I've ever had a rooster for an alarm clock," Cadin admitted.

"Are you a city girl?" Terri teased.

"Yes, ma'am, I was born and raised in the concrete jungle, what about you?"

"Pure country," she answered. "Until a few weeks ago we lived in a small town in Florida called Quincy."

"I've heard of that. Isn't it just outside of Tallahassee?"

"That would be the place. We lived on a small peanut farm."

"So you're probably used to Roscoe then?"

"Yes, but his name was Buford."

Cadin smiled and took a sip of coffee.

"I hope you like over easy, I forgot to ask," Miss Betty said as she placed a plate of food in front of her.

"That's perfect," Cadin said as she took a fork and started mashing up the eggs.

Both Terri and Miss Betty started laughing.

Cadin looked up at them confused.

"That's exactly what Lexie does with her eggs," Terri said.

"Ah okay, I thought I was doing something forbidden for a second."

"Nope, just tickled by the coincidence," Miss Betty answered.

Terri checked her watch. "I better get a move on. See y'all later today," she said.

"Have a good one," Cadin called after her as she swallowed a bite of food.

"What are your plans for today, Cadin?"

"I want to ride around the area and do a few errands and then I'm coming back to help Lexie harvest some pecans."

"Oh, she'll love that," Miss Betty said.

"Good morning, ladies," Sister Frances said as she entered the room.

"Are you ready for some breakfast?" Miss Betty asked.

"I'm actually hungry this morning, so yes, please."

26

Miss Betty looked at Cadin. "Is there anything else I can get you?"

"No, ma'am, I'm good here. That was delicious. Thank you."

"My pleasure," Miss Betty said as she walked into the kitchen.

Sister Frances poured a cup of coffee. "Do you need a refill?"

"Yes, I think I can handle one more."

"Sit tight and I'll bring the pot over," she said.

She filled Cadin's cup and offered her the cream and sugar. She also handed her a folded piece of paper. "The information you asked about last night," she said.

Cadin took the paper and placed it in her pocket. "Thank you."

She drank another cup of coffee while Sister Frances ate. "I'll be back in a few hours. If you will let Lexie know we'll work on harvesting when I return, I'd appreciate that."

"No problem. She'll sleep at least another hour and then I'll get some breakfast into her," Miss Betty said.

"I'll see you ladies later then," Cadin said and left the house.

She walked to the covered area and pushed her bike around to the front of the house before she started it to keep from waking the others. She took out the slip of paper to read the address and the simple instructions Sister Frances had written down for her. As she rode through town, she noted the location of the bank that she would pay a visit to later that morning.

She located the small farmhouse and smiled as she pulled into the drive and parked. It was a quaint little home, probably three bedrooms at most, obviously maintained with loving care. Beautiful roses were in bloom in the immaculate flowerbeds. The lawn was in need of mowing, but otherwise the grounds were in good shape. She walked up the short sidewalk and frowned when she reached the door to find the foreclosure announcement posted on the door. Cadin looked around but could not find a For Sale sign posted anywhere. *That's a good sign. It's not on the market yet.*

She walked the length of the porch, peering into windows at the bare interior. Apparently, Miss Betty removed the furnishings and her personal belongings when evicted. *She must have them in storage somewhere.*

Cadin continued around the house peering in windows. At the back of the property she found a large detached garage and workshop. She was surprised to find the door unlocked. *This must have been Henry's haven.* The tools and gardening supplies were still inside the building. She returned outside and behind the building found a large fenced garden spot. Weeds had taken over the vegetable plants, which made her frown. Someone had taken great care to plant and tend the garden in the past and it was sad to see the fertile garden go to waste.

*This simply will not do.* Another idea popped into her head. She would need help with the project, but she had the perfect little helper in mind. *First things first, though,* she thought and pulled out her cell phone.

A white wooden swing hung in the backyard and Cadin took a seat while she dialed Pam's number. When Pam answered, Cadin told her of her plans.

Pam could hear the excitement in Cadin's voice. "I think it's a lovely plan. Let me know if you need any help."

"I'm glad you agree," she told her friend. "Don't be surprised if the bank contacts you today about a check being written out of state, because I intend to start this process today."

When she ended the call, she walked around the house to her bike. "It's time to see a banker," she spoke aloud.

†

After parking in the bank's lot, Cadin reached into her saddlebag and pulled out a business card. She confirmed that her checkbook was in her back pocket.

An elderly man was exiting the bank as she reached the door. He smiled and hurried through the door, opening it for her. "Here you go, ma'am."

"Why thank you, kind sir," she said and flashed him her most brilliant smile. "Have a great day."

"You too, ma'am," he said as he tipped his hat to her.

She walked into the bank, went straight to the reception area, and handed the woman her card. "I would like to speak to the bank president," she said.

"Do you have an appointment, Miss..." she looked at Cadin's card, "Miss Michaels."

"No, ma'am, I don't, but I am here to buy a house, so maybe he can make a few minutes for me," she said with a sweet smile.

"Have a seat and let me make an inquiry," she said and scuttled away from her desk as Cadin found a comfortable seat. She could see the woman through a glass window as she approached a man she assumed was the president and handed him her card. The man looked at the card and immediately sat up in his chair and straightened his tie. The woman scurried from his office and approached her.

"Mr. Thomas will see you now, Miss Michaels. May I get you something to drink?"

"No, ma'am, but thank you for asking," she said politely, following the woman to the office.

"George Thomas," the man said as he offered her his hand.

"Cadin Michaels, pleased to meet you, Mr. Thomas."

"Oh please, just call me George. Won't you have a seat?" he said, gesturing to the chair across from his desk.

Cadin settled onto the plush chair and looked up at the man.

"What may I do for you this morning?" he asked.

"I am here to buy a house," she said, leaning forward to remove her checkbook from her back pocket. "May I borrow a pen?"

George's eyes grew wide, but managed to hand her a pen. "What house are you interested in?"

Without looking up from her checkbook, she reached into her pocket and handed him the slip of paper Sister Frances had given her with the address written on it. "This one. I believe it's a recent foreclosure from the notice plastered on the front door," she said as she busied herself writing out a check.

He looked at the address. "This would be the Franklin place," he said after checking his files.

"Yes, that's the one. I believe you foreclosed on the property for a bit over twenty thousand dollars after Mr. Franklin died."

"Yes, his death was unfortunate, and his account was several months behind. I'm afraid his widow had no way to bring the account current," he said. "Business is business."

"It is a sad day in America when a woman of her stature is forced to live in a women's shelter after she is ruthlessly evicted from the only place she's known as home," Cadin said, her voice lowered to a growl. "You know damned well you could have extended her the courtesy to wait for her benefits to come in so she could refinance the home with you." She ripped the check out of her checkbook and placed it on the desk in front of him.

George, genuinely startled by her movements and the edge in her voice asked, "What's this?"

"It is a check made out to your establishment for twenty-five thousand dollars," she said. "The amount should cover her remaining debt, the expenses for the paperwork and deed registry of the property. I would like the deed registered to the Missy Foundation."

"Now wait just a minute," he cried, his voice louder than he intended.

Activity in the bank came to a halt and she could feel the eyes of the bank employees and customers drawn to the office.

Cadin watched as redness crept up his neck into his face. "Why would I sell you the place for this amount?" he snarled at her. "That house is worth so much more."

"First, the housing market is flooded with homes that are not selling. Second, you haven't listed the property for sale yet, so the foreclosure paperwork isn't final." She looked up to see his eyes bugging out. "Third, you will never sell the property after I raise a terrible scandal about another heartless banker stealing a lifetime home from a widow. It's a shame a banker takes more pride in making a sale than taking care of his lifelong customers."

"Now hold on here a minute," he started, but Cadin cut off his argument.

"It's a more than a fair offer and I shouldn't think it would take more than three days to secure the paperwork. You can reach me at the number on my card," Cadin said and stood to leave.

George's mouth was hanging open as he stood behind his desk.

"Do you have any questions?" she asked.

"No," he stammered.

"I will assume we have a deal then and I will wait to hear from you soon, George," she said sweetly and offered him her hand.

"Yes, yes, we'll be in touch," he answered, and then collapsed back into his chair.

"Thank you and good day, sir," she said and walked out of his office, all eyes in the bank following her movement. She looked at her watch and grinned. "Fifteen minutes, that has to be some sort of record." Still smiling, she mounted her bike and rode to a nearby store where she purchased several pairs of inexpensive shorts and a pair of sneakers. She placed her purchases in the saddlebags and rode back to Sister Frances's home.

☩

Lexie was riding a bicycle in the yard when she pulled into the drive. Cadin parked under the cover and took her bags from the saddlebags. Lexie rushed over to her and Cadin asked, "Ready to gather some nuts?"

"Yes, ma'am," Lexie squealed.

"Let me change clothes and we'll get started." Cadin walked into the sleeping area and changed into the shorts and sneakers. When she walked back out Lexie was patiently waiting for her. "Got your bucket?" Cadin asked.

"Yes, ma'am," she answered.

"Let's see if we can find a rake and we'll get started. Do you know if Sister Frances has a rake?"

"There's one in a small tool shed out back," Lexie answered.

"Let's go get it and start to work."

†

Lexie kneeled on the ground and began picking up pecans as Cadin started raking them into piles for her. It took little time to fill her first bucket. Lexie carried it to Sister Frances to empty it and she came rushing back out to the orchard.

When she came back out, Cadin stopped raking. "I have another project I need your help with, but it's a secret," she said.

Lexie's eyes sparkled when she heard the word "secret," and asked, "What is it?"

"There is a garden not far from here that I need help cleaning up and I thought I might hire you to help."

"What will we be doing?" Lexie asked as she began picking up pecans.

"It's going to be hard work, pulling weeds, trimming plants and maybe picking some veggies," Cadin said.

"I can do all that," Lexie said. "I'll have to ask Mommy though."

"I understand. I'll talk to her when she gets home if you'd like."

"She will probably have some questions. Why is it a secret?" she asked.

"Because it is a surprise for Miss Betty," she explained. "I don't want her to know what we're doing until I know something for sure."

"Okay," Lexie said, but Cadin could see she didn't quite understand.

33

"Just don't mention it to anyone but your mommy," Cadin said.

"Yes ma'am," Lexie said.

The back door of the kitchen opened and Miss Betty stepped outside and yelled, "Lunchtime."

"I'm starved," Cadin said. "Let's eat."

Lexie picked up her bucket and carried it proudly to the house.

Sister Frances saw Lexie carrying the bucket and smiled, "Another one already?"

"Yes, ma'am, it goes faster when I have help," Lexie said.

"I see that," Sister Frances said with a wink to Cadin. "You two go clean up and come eat and I'll dump your bucket."

"Yes, ma'am," Lexie said and handed her the bucket.

She and Lexie walked into the bathroom and washed their hands and faces. "Eww, we were dirty," Cadin said, surprised by the amount of dust they washed from their faces.

"Yes, we were," she agreed.

They walked into the dining room to find a large stack of ham sandwiches on the table and a bowl filled with chips.

"Tea for two hard workers," Miss Betty said as she brought glasses to the table.

She and Sister Frances joined them at the table with another mother and a small boy named Tommy. "You two have been working up a storm this morning," Sister Frances said.

"We've got to get the harvest done," Cadin said.

"Have you counted?" she asked Lexie.

Lexie looked shocked. "No, ma'am. I was so busy filling the bucket I forgot to count."

Sister Frances chuckled. "That's okay. Miss Betty and I will count. I think we need to do some shelling this afternoon, Betty."

"We'd better if we're to have any ready for the market next weekend."

"Speaking of weekends," Sister Frances said, "could I ask a favor of you, Cadin?"

"Sure thing, what can I do?"

"Miss Betty and I need a chauffeur and a chaperone this Saturday night."

"Well, that certainly sounds interesting," Cadin said. "You have my attention."

"A friend of ours holds an annual, women only dove hunt once a year. It's this Saturday night. We'd like to go, but neither of us sees well after dark."

"A dove hunt at night, that sounds suspicious."

"No silly, the hunt is during the day and then a big cookout is held. There's often as many as four generations present and it's the only time we can see some of our older friends," Miss Betty said.

"You ever been yard porchin'?" Sister Frances asked.

"Since I have no idea what you just said, I'll have to answer no," Cadin said.

"Yard porchin' is what we country folks do in the fall when the weather turns nice. My friend has a large deck out in her yard and this is where the party people go," Sister Frances said.

"The younger crowd will pull a big screen television out and run the cable connection out the window so they can drink beer and watch SEC football, while the rest of us cook and prepare a meal fit for a king," Sister Frances said.

"That sounds too good to pass up," Cadin said. "What's the dress code?"

"There is none," Miss Betty said.

"We go naked?" Cadin teased.

"No, child, people will be dressed in all kinds of outfits. A lot of orange and blue and crimson as you might expect, but there's no telling who will wear the most outlandish outfit." Miss Betty smiled. "Your jeans and a T-shirt will be just fine."

"Yard porchin' it is then. What time do we need to be there?"

"Women usually start coming in around lunch, so there will be sandwiches and such and those that want to hunt, well they hunt," Sister Frances said.

"Is there really any hunting going on or is this an excuse for a party?"

"Oh there are shotguns and generally a few shots are fired; I think we even had a few birds shot down a couple of years ago," Miss Betty said.

Cadin turned and looked at Lexie. "May I have the afternoon off Saturday?"

Lexie giggled. "Yes, you can."

"We should ask Terri if she would like to join us after she gets off work and take Lexie with us. It would be a way for her to start meeting new friends," Sister Frances said.

"That sounds like fun. Will you ask Mommy if I can go?"

"I sure will," Sister Frances said.

"Eat up so we can get back to work," Cadin said.

†

After a significant number of the sandwiches disappeared, Lexie retrieved her bucket and they returned to work. By midafternoon, Lexie had filled six buckets and was working on another when Miss Betty brought out a pitcher of lemonade.

"You two need to take a break," she said and poured drinks.

Sitting on a small bench drinking the refreshing lemonade was where Terri found them when she arrived home from work. Lexie waved to her mom, who came over to check on their progress. "How's it going?" she asked.

"It's been awesome today," Lexie said. "Having Cadin rake the pecans really helps."

Terri looked up at Cadin and smiled. "Thanks for helping Lexie."

"She's done all the hard work, I've just raked."

Miss Betty picked up the pitcher and looked at Terri.

"I believe Sister Frances has something she wants to ask you," Miss Betty said.

"Okay, I'll go see what she wants and then shower and relax for a little while. I want you to finish up here soon so you can get cleaned up for supper, okay?"

"Can we work another hour, Mom?" Lexie asked.

Terri looked at Cadin who nodded her head. "Yes, but not a minute more, you're dusty from head to foot."

"Let's go, Cadin," Lexie said and ran back to her bucket.

"I have something to ask you too, but it will wait until later," Cadin said as she bent to pick up the rake.

Terri nodded and headed for the house, emerging several minutes later to give Lexie the thumbs-up sign. "Looks like we're going to a party," Cadin said with a grin.

†

When the hour was up, Lexie took her final bucket into the house and dumped it into the large garbage can Sister Frances had set out for her. Then she ran back outside to store her bucket. "We almost filled the garbage can today," she said with excitement.

"We'll get it tomorrow," Cadin said as she opened the shed to return her rake. Her eyes landed on a shop vac and the gears of her imagination started turning. "Let's hit the showers, boss," she said, then followed Lexie to the sleeping area.

†

After cleaning the dinner dishes, Cadin asked Terri and Lexie to go outside with her for a few minutes. Finding a small bench by the orchard the trio sat and Cadin turned toward Terri. "I asked Lexie if she would work with me on a special project, with pay of course, and I need to ask your permission and for your assistance."

"What did you have in mind?" Terri asked.

"I made an offer today to buy Miss Betty's house from the bank. I will know by Wednesday, but they would be foolish to refuse the offer. I also went by the house before going to the bank and there is a very nice garden plot, but the weeds have overgrown the plants. I was hoping Lexie could help me clear it later this week."

Terri's mouth hung open. When she was finally able to speak, she said, "That is really nice of you. Of course Lexie can help, and I'm off Thursday and Friday so I'll help too."

"I could have keys to the house by then. Maybe you could do some cleaning on the inside while we work on the garden," Cadin suggested. "I peeked in the windows and it doesn't look bad. Maybe some dusting and mopping of floors."

"I would be glad to do that," Terri said, wearing a huge grin.

"This has to be kept a secret between the three of us," Cadin said. "I'd hate to get her hopes up and the deal falls through."

"Oh Cadin, Miss Betty is going to be so happy," Terri said with tears in her eyes.

"She deserved better treatment than what she got and I made sure the bank president knew that before I left his office this morning," she said with a grin. "So here's the plan. I think Lexie and I can knock out the pecan harvest by Wednesday if we work hard, and then we can start on Miss Betty's place."

"When will you tell her?" Lexie asked.

"I'm not sure yet. I was thinking of waiting until we finished our projects. What do you think?"

"I think you should tell her as soon as you know something definite," Terri said. "She needs something to lift her spirits, besides no one cleans a home better than the owner."

"You make a good point. As soon as I sign the paperwork and get the keys I will come back to tell her."

"This is incredible," Terri said. "Thank you for doing this for her."

"That's not quite all," she said. "There is one special condition that I know she will agree to in a heartbeat."

Terri's brow wrinkled in a frown. "What is it?"

"The house has three bedrooms in it, and I would request that you and Lexie be allowed to live there until you have saved enough for a place of your own. You would pay her one hundred dollars a week, of which fifty would be put in a savings account for you toward a down payment."

Terri's hand flew to her mouth. Tears started to flow down her cheeks.

"Would you be agreeable with that arrangement?"

"Oh my goodness, yes," Terri said.

"Fine, that's all set then."

Lexie climbed into Cadin's lap and looked up at her. "We would have a real house again?"

"Yes, you would," she answered.

Lexie wrapped her arms around Cadin and hugged her tightly. "Thank you, Cadin. Isn't this great, Mommy?"

"Yes, it is wonderful news. Thank you, Cadin."

"You're very welcome."

"I have to ask something though," Terri said.

Cadin smiled, knowing the question she was about to be asked. "You want to know why, don't you?"

"Yes, why would you be so generous to complete strangers?"

It was Cadin's turn to tear up. "The woman I told you about last night, my girlfriend, Missy, was a social worker who devoted her life to helping others. After she died I sued the hospital and the physician who killed her and used the settlement to fund a foundation in her name." She stopped long enough to take a breath. "I will use the money to help out as many women in need as I can. You three will be the first recipients of funds from the Missy Foundation."

"I am so sorry for your loss. She sounds like she was a special woman."

"She was the best I could ever hope for," she said, looking away to wipe a tear away from her cheek.

"It makes what you're doing for us even that much more special."

"Missy would have done this, so I take comfort in knowing what I'm trying to do would make her happy."

Terri leaned over and kissed Cadin's cheek. "She was lucky to have you."

"I was the lucky one," she answered.

When Terri left to get Lexie to bed, Cadin stayed behind and looked up the stars for a while longer. With a deep sigh, she looked up and said, "If you're listening, I hope you approve."

A warm breeze blew up unexpectedly. She felt it wrapping around her body like a lover's embrace, and she smiled, knowing Missy was listening. "Goodnight, my love," she said and walked inside.

# Chapter Three

Lexie was up eating breakfast with her mother when Cadin walked in the next morning. "Good morning, ladies," Cadin said when she entered. "You're up early, Lexie."

"We have lots of work to do today," she said.

"Yes, we do, so eat a good breakfast."

"What can I get you?" Miss Betty asked from the kitchen.

Cadin looked at what Lexie was munching, "I think I'll have some Tony the Tiger too."

"One bowl coming up," Miss Betty said. "Coffee too?"

"Yes, please."

Terri watched her daughter attack the bowl of cereal. "She's been up for an hour. I'm surprised she didn't wake you."

"She must have been as quiet as a church mouse. I didn't hear a thing."

Sister Frances was sitting at the end of the table shelling pecans. "I think we will use some of these nuts to bake some pies today. Does that sound good?"

"You have my mouth watering already," Cadin said.

"You are racking up a nice paycheck on these nuts, Lexie," Sister Frances said.

Lexie looked up from her bowl and smiled, a milk mustache forming on her upper lip. "Just wait till you see how many we get today," she said.

"We better get to cracking then, Miss Betty. Pun intended," Sister Frances said as the others started laughing.

"Okay, I'm off to work. Have a good day, honey," Terri said and bent down to kiss the top of Lexie's head.

"You too, Mommy."

After Terri left, Cadin looked at Sister Frances. "I noticed there is a shop vac out in the shed. Does it work?"

"The last time I checked it did, why?" she asked.

"I was thinking I could rake the pecans like we have been and Lexie could suck them up with the shop vac," Cadin said.

"Well I'll be danged, that's a good idea," Sister Frances said. "Even if some of them get cracked while getting sucked up, that will save me some cracking too."

"Let's give it a shot then, Lexie. What do you think?" Cadin asked.

"Let's do it," she said and carried her empty bowl into the kitchen and handed it to Miss Betty. "Thanks," she said.

"You're welcome," Miss Betty said. "Did you get enough?"

"Yes, ma'am," Lexie said, rubbing her stomach.

"I guess I'd better get a move on then," Cadin said and returned to her cereal bowl.

✝

Cadin pulled out the shop vac, rinsed the inside of the canister, and dried it before attaching the hose. "You think you can handle this?" she asked.

"I'm pretty sure I can," Lexie answered with a smile. She located several long extension cords, plugged one into a power outlet, and then started stretching it out toward the orchard. "Here, you take these and keep walking and I'll grab the shop vac."

Lexie took the cord and Cadin picked up the shop vac and her rake and followed the child into the orchard. When they reached the spot where they had stopped the previous day, Cadin set down the vac and plugged it in. "Let's make up a pile and we can see if this works."

Cadin went to work with the rake and when she had a sizeable pile, she returned to Lexie. "Let's give it a shot," she said and handed Lexie the end of the hose. "Ready?"

Lexie nodded her head and Cadin flipped the power switch. The vac roared to life and the pecans startled rattling through the hose. After a few seconds, she cut the power and Lexie looked up at her. "Let's check the canister to see how the nuts made it." Cadin released the lid and they peered inside the canister. A few of the nuts had cracked, but they made it through the hose in good shape. Cadin held her hand out to Lexie. "Gimme five," she said. Lexie slapped her palm and they went back to work.

✝

Her idea worked out well and it didn't take long for the tank to fill with nuts. "I think I better carry this one," Cadin said as they removed the canister lid and carried the nuts to the dining room.

Sister Frances chuckled and shook her head. "If you ever have thoughts of giving up your law practice, I think you'd have a great career as a pecan harvester," she told Cadin.

Lexie's chest filled with pride as the canister nearly filled the garbage can. "Get to cracking," she told Sister Frances.

"She is such a slave driver," Miss Betty said as she eyed their work.

"We have to finish this soon," Lexie said.

"Oh, why is that?" Miss Betty asked.

Cadin watched as Lexie realized she might have blundered, but when Lexie spoke, she realized the kid had smarts. "Because Cadin has promised me a ride on her bike when we finish," she said. "Let's go, Cadin."

As they stepped outside, she smiled at Lexie and said, "That was quick thinking."

"I thought I'd messed up for a second."

"I think she bought it," Cadin said. "Let's get cracking."

Lexie chuckled and waited for Cadin to fasten the lid to the canister. "She's all yours, captain," Cadin said and saluted her.

✝

They emptied the canister four more times before Miss Betty called them in for a lunch of grilled cheese sandwiches and tomato soup.

"I haven't had this combination since I was a little girl," Cadin said. "This is perfect."

"You two are working hard," Miss Betty said.

Sister Frances and another woman were shelling the pecans. "Just when we think we've made a dent in this pile you bring in another canister," she said.

"We've got it going on," Cadin said in a singsong voice.

"That you do, my friend," Sister Frances said.

"How about I cook some fried chicken and mashed potatoes tonight to go with the pecan pies?" Miss Betty asked.

"Can we have some corn too?" Lexie asked.

Miss Betty asked, "On or off the cob?"

"Off please," Lexie said.

"I think that can be arranged," she answered.

"Awesome," Lexie said with a grin.

Cadin finished her soup and carried the bowl to the kitchen. Lexie was still eating her soup. "I'm going to get a head start on you, but take your time and finish that soup."

"Yes, ma'am," Lexie said.

†

Cadin checked her cell phone to make sure she hadn't missed a call from the bank. Her screen was blank. *It's only been a day, tomorrow will tell all.* She really hadn't given much thought to what steps she would take if good ole George turned down her offer. He did shake on the deal, but she knew he was in a state of shock when he did so. Only time will tell, she thought as she picked up the rake.

She had two large piles raked when Lexie flew out of the house and started up the shop vac. Cadin smiled and went back to raking.

✝

When Terri arrived home hours later, she was amazed at the amount of progress Lexie and Cadin had made. "Is there anything I can do to help?"

"I could use something to drink, Mommy," Lexie said.

"That does sound good and we'll take a break," Cadin said. "We've done a lot today."

Lexie grinned. "Yes, we have."

"It looks like you've come up with a drastic improvement on collecting the nuts," Terri said, nodding toward the shop vac.

"A brainstorm, if I say so myself," Cadin said.

"Smart move," Terri said and walked to the house to get them drinks.

"Let's go crash on the bench," Cadin said.

"Fine with me," Lexie answered.

Cadin could see her young partner was rapidly losing energy and decided they would soon call it quits for the day.

Terri brought them glasses of tea and sat with them on the bench. "How much longer do you plan on working?"

"You have to ask the boss," Cadin said and looked at Lexie.

"Not much longer, Mommy, I'm getting tired."

"Why don't you go get a shower and take a quick nap before dinner? You were up really early this morning," Terri said.

Lexie looked up at Cadin. "You go ahead. I will finish up here and put our tools away. You did a good job today," Cadin said.

Lexie quickly corrected her. "We did good."

"Yes, we did," she said.

Lexie finished her drink and handed the glass to Terri. "Off to the shower with you."

"Yes, ma'am; I'll see you at supper, Cadin."

"Save me some hot water," Cadin teased.

"I will," Lexie said and headed to the sleeping quarters.

"She's really fond of you. I hope you know that," Cadin smiled. "She's a good kid."

"Thanks, she's my pride and joy."

"You should be very proud then. I'd love to have a daughter like her one day."

"Only time will tell," Terri said. "You all done?" she asked, reaching for Cadin's tea glass.

"Yes, thanks."

"See you later then," Terri said.

†

Cadin went back to work and was busy raking when Terri showed up carrying a rake. "Your partner is sleeping, so I thought I would help you for a bit."

"Thanks, I'd like to get a start on this last row."

"You know I couldn't wipe the smile from my face today after the news you gave us last night," Terri said as she began raking.

"I hope to hear from the bank tomorrow," Cadin said. "Hopefully early morning, so we can make this final."

"Will you come by the store and let me know?" she asked.

"May I bring Lexie with me?"

"You certainly may," she said.

"You have a deal then."

They raked for another hour before Cadin finally said, "I think we've done enough for today, I'm bushed."

"Go enjoy a nice hot shower and I'll put the tools away for the night," Terri said.

Cadin smiled a tired smile. "Thanks, I'd appreciate that."

†

The shower worked magic in relieving the weariness from Cadin's body. When she finally emerged from the shower and dressed in clean clothes, she felt revitalized and hungry. She looked at her watch and smiled. "Time to eat."

She was the last to arrive in the dining room. The women were bustling around preparing to serve the meal when she walked inside. "There you are. We were starting to get worried," Miss Betty teased. "Have a seat and we will be ready in just a few minutes."

"Yes, ma'am." Cadin took a seat at the table. Less than a minute later, she jumped when her cell phone vibrated in her pocket. She pulled it out to find she had missed a call from the bank. Fortunately, there was a voice mail. "I'll be right back," she said and stepped outside. She took a deep breath and pushed the button to listen to the message. The smile on her face grew wider as the woman stated she was calling to set up a time for a closing on the house she was buying and would appreciate Cadin giving her a return call first thing in the morning.

Terri caught her eye when Cadin walked back into the room. The smile on Cadin's face told her she had gotten good news. She returned the smile and then went back to preparing a plate for Lexie.

"This meal smells terrific," Cadin said as Terri handed her a plate with a healthy portion of fried chicken, mashed potatoes with gravy, and a mound of sweet corn.

Cadin took her plate to the table and waited for the others to take their seats. They joined hands while Sister Frances blessed the meal and then she and Lexie hungrily attacked the food.

Between bites, Cadin looked up at Sister Frances and asked, "Who would you recommend to cater a meal?"

"Cater, here in Greensboro? My child, did you get too much sun today?" she teased.

"Okay, let me rephrase, where can I go to get a meal big enough to feed us?"

"I'd recommend the BBQ spot on the edge of town. They make great pulled pork and ribs. Are you tired of our cooking already?"

"No, ma'am, the food here is to die for, but tomorrow night we are having a celebration," she said.

Every fork at the table stopped in midstream as heads turned to look at her. "What are we celebrating?" Sister Frances asked.

"Can't say," Cadin said. "It's a surprise."

"Oh great, now we won't sleep a wink tonight," Miss Betty teased.

"I would recommend getting a good night's rest. We have plenty of work to do ahead of us," Cadin teased back.

"You are cruel, Cadin Michaels," Terri said with a chuckle.

Cadin just smiled and took another large bite of chicken. When she swallowed, she turned back to Sister Frances. "Will you take me to this BBQ place tomorrow in your car?"

"I'd be delighted," she answered.

Cadin fought off all attempts to get a clue to what she was up to throughout the rest of the meal, but she easily dodged all the probing questions.

When they finished the meal, Miss Betty and Sister Frances carried plates and three delicious-looking pecan pies to the table. "Who would like coffee?" Miss Betty asked. She took orders and returned to the kitchen as Sister Frances started slicing and serving the pie.

†

"I take it you got the news you were expecting?" Terri asked after the kitchen was cleaned and she had joined Cadin and Lexie for a walk.

"I got a voice mail from the bank wanting to set up a time to close on the house," she answered with a huge grin. "Hopefully, by tomorrow night, we will have keys to your new home."

"That is going to be so exciting. I love your idea about a celebration tomorrow night too. It will be a very special treat for all of us and give Miss Betty and Sister Frances a break from cooking."

"I will give the bank a call as soon as they open in the morning," Cadin said as she held the door open for them.

Terri asked, "Will you two work before you call or wait until you have more information?"

"That depends on the boss lady. If she gets up early again, we can get some work done before going to the bank," she said with a wink to Lexie.

"Will you make sure I'm up early, Mommy?" Lexie asked. "I want us to finish tomorrow so we can start on the garden."

"I will wake you up once I'm dressed for work. Is that early enough?"

"Yes, ma'am," Lexie answered.

Terri smiled at her daughter with pride. "Get those teeth brushed and your pajamas on and I'll tuck you in."

Cadin changed clothes and joined Lexie in the bathroom to brush her teeth. "I'm going to sleep like a log tonight," she told the smiling child. "I'm whipped."

"Me too," Lexie said, rubbing her tired eyes.

She climbed into the bed and looked over to see Lexie tucked under her covers. "Goodnight, boss," she said.

Lexie looked at her with a grin. "Goodnight, Cadin."

†

After breakfast, Cadin and Lexie took their tools from the shed and went to work. Cadin set her alarm on vibrate for nine to remind her to call the bank and slipped it into her pocket. There was half a row left to rake and she tackled the challenge while Lexie started collecting the pecans. She was determined to finish the project today so they could begin work on Miss Betty's garden tomorrow.

When the phone vibrated in her pocket, Cadin pulled it out to silence the alarm then dialed the number for the bank.

The woman who answered the phone put her directly through to the loan officer who said she had the paperwork ready for signing. Pleased, Cadin agreed to an appointment at three to close on the house. That would give her plenty of time to finish the pecan harvest, close on the house and be ready to feast with the others where she would make her announcement.

"We're all set," she said to Lexie with a grin. She placed the phone back in her pocket and carried the canister inside to empty it before returning to her raking.

✝

They emptied the last canister and put away their tools at noon. Miss Betty had sandwiches and chips waiting for them after they washed their hands.

"What are you two going to do now that you are finished harvesting?" Sister Frances asked.

"I have another project I need Lexie's help with. We are going to take a look at it after we shower and dress in some clean clothes," Cadin said. "We'll be back in plenty time to get the BBQ," she added.

"Good, I've already called in the order and they promise to have it ready by a quarter past five," Sister Frances said.

"Good deal," Cadin said as she finished her sandwich. "Ready to get cleaned up?" she asked Lexie.

"Yes, ma'am," she said as she drained her drink.

"We'll be back later today," she said as they left the dining room.

"We need to shower and put some jeans on," she told Lexie.

Lexie smiled up at her. "I know. Mommy has already laid my clothes out for me."

"Cool."

Terri had laid out a pair of jeans and green T-shirt for Lexie. She also had a pair of cowboy boots and socks placed on the bed. "That should do nicely," she said as they stripped out of their work clothes and walked to the showers.

†

Cadin pulled out her spare helmet and did her best to tighten it on Lexie's head. As she feared, it was way too large, but it would have to work for now. She straddled the bike and then told Lexie how to climb onto the back of the bike.

"All set?" she asked. "Would you like to see the house before we go see your mom?"

"Yes, ma'am," Lexie said.

"Hold on tight then," she said and smiled when Lexie's tiny arms circled her waist. Cadin started the bike and drove it out to the street. She drove carefully, winding her way through downtown, past the bank, to Miss Betty's house and parked in front.

†

Lexie's mouth was hanging open when she turned the bike off. "This is beautiful," she said. "I can't believe we can actually live here."

"Very soon, you will have your own room," Cadin said as she unbuckled the helmet. "Want to look around?"

54

Lexie took her hand and they stepped onto the front porch. She peeked through the windows and when they walked around to the back of the house, Cadin lifted her up to look through the higher windows.

"Wow, this is awesome," she said as Cadin placed her down on the ground.

"Want to see the garden and our next project?"

Lexie nodded excitedly and followed her behind the garage. She frowned when she saw the overgrowth of the garden.

"Relax it's not as bad as it looks. We can handle this."

"If you say so, Cadin," she said with a doubtful look on her face.

"Trust me on this. Let's go see your mom and then ride to the bank."

† 

It only took a few minutes to find Terri, busy stocking the cereal shelves.

She looked up to see them approaching and smiled. "Hey there you two, I take it you have good news."

"The closing is at three," Cadin said.

"Cadin took me by the house, and it's so cool, Mom, you're going to love it," Lexie said.

Terri ruffled her daughter's hair. "I'm sure I will, sweetheart. Did you finish your harvesting today?"

Lexie looked up at her wearing a proud smile. "Yes, ma'am, we did. Sister Frances said she was going to have to rob a bank to pay me." Lexie looked at her mom with a confused look. "She won't really, will she Mom?"

"No, honey, that's just an expression. It means you made a lot of money."

"Cool," Lexie said.

"Would you mind if Lexie goes to the bank with me or would you rather I take her home?" Cadin asked.

Terri looked at Lexie patiently awaiting her answer. "I don't see why she can't go with you."

Lexie hugged her mom. "Thanks, Mommy, I'm having so much fun riding Cadin's bike."

"You just continue to hang on tight," Terri said.

"No worries there, Lexie's got a death grip on my waist," Cadin said.

Terri smiled. "I guess I will see you back at Sister Frances's then."

"See you soon," Cadin said and turned to walk back to her bike with Lexie in tow. "Let's go buy a house," she said as she straddled the bike and offered Lexie her hand.

"Let's do it," Lexie said as she took Cadin's hand and scrambled onto the bike.

†

Elizabeth, the loan officer, met Cadin and Lexie at the receptionist's desk. Cadin glanced toward George's office and when he saw her looking at him, he dropped his head back to the document he was reviewing. She smiled and followed Elizabeth back to the cubicle and helped Lexie into a seat, then sat across from Elizabeth.

"This is a very fast closing," Elizabeth said. "I've never had a deal move this quickly."

"I offered George a deal too good to be true," Cadin said.

"You must have. He can be pretty tough to deal with," she whispered.

Cadin smiled. "You just have to know how to work him."

"Remind me to give you a call the next time I want to buy a house."

"I'd be delighted to help you negotiate," Cadin answered.

"Well let's get to it."

†

For the next forty-five minutes, Elizabeth explained each document then Cadin signed each page. She was about to get writer's cramp from signing her name when Elizabeth announced the document in her hand was the last.

"Now all I need to do is package up your copies of the documents and hand you the keys to your new home."

Cadin turned to Lexie and held her hand up for a high five. "We've done it," she said.

Elizabeth handed Cadin a thick manila envelope and a set of keys. "Congratulations," she said and offered Cadin her hand.

"Thanks," she said and turned to Lexie. "Let's go celebrate."

"All right," Lexie said and followed her out of the bank.

She placed the paperwork in her saddlebags and handed Lexie the keys. "Slip these into your pocket," she said.

Lexie crammed the keys deep into her pocket and then waited for Cadin to fasten the helmet.

Cadin checked her watch. They'd made good time inside the bank. "Want to go look at the inside?"

"Yes," Lexie said.

"Okay, let's ride."

✝

She took the keys from Lexie and opened the front door. Reaching for a switch she flipped it up and was surprised when the lights came on. She would ask Miss Betty to call and transfer the utilities to her name tomorrow or the next day. "This is really nice," she said as she followed Lexie through the house.

"It's so big," Lexie said, her eyes growing wide with delight.

"It will be perfect for the three of you."

They walked through the entire house and Cadin was pleased to find that the interior was in good shape and shouldn't take much to clean. When they walked back outside, she handed Lexie the keys. "Lock her up," she said.

Lexie took the keys and turned the lock. She looked up at Cadin who said, "You keep them."

Lexie smiled and tucked them away in her pocket.

✝

When they arrived home, they found everyone sitting around the dining room tables shelling pecans.

"You've made a good dent in those today," Cadin said as she slid in beside Sister Frances.

"You two worked so hard to collect them, we had to start shelling to get ready for the market next week. Miss

Betty counted them for us and I owe you forty dollars, Lexie."

"Wow," Lexie said.

Cadin wasn't sure Lexie comprehended how much money that really was, but Lexie would have been happy if it were ten dollars.

"I'll go to the bank tomorrow and get your money, if that's okay with you," Sister Frances said.

"That's fine, Sister Frances," Lexie said. "You really don't need to pay me after all you've done for Mommy and me."

Terri's chest swelled with pride at her daughter's comment. She was growing up way too fast.

"Nonsense, we had a deal and you've earned every penny of the money," Sister Frances said.

Cadin also smiled proudly at Lexie's behavior. "What can we do to help?"

Sister Frances looked at the clock to find they had a half hour before they would leave to pick up supper. "Will you and Lexie start filling those bags for us? Unbroken halves in one bag and pieces in another?"

"I think we can handle that," Cadin said. "You want wholes or pieces?"

Lexie thought for a second. "I'll take the pieces," she answered.

Cadin took out two Ziploc bags and opened one for each of them. "Let's do it."

They filled bags while the others continued to shell. When it was time to leave, Sister Frances turned to Cadin. "Are you ready to go?"

"Yes ma'am, I am."

"The others will clean up here and set the tables for dinner, so if you're ready, let's go."

Cadin followed Sister Frances out to the car and climbed in the passenger seat. Sister Frances slid in behind the wheel and turned to Cadin. "I don't know what you are up to, but I have the feeling you are going to spring some big news on us tonight."

"You're right, I am," Cadin said. "You will find out within the hour."

"You are a difficult woman," Sister Frances said with a smile. She started the car and pulled out of the drive.

†

When they returned, Terri and Miss Betty came out to help carry in the bags of food and spread it out on the table. After everyone took their seats, Sister Frances gave thanks for the feast before them.

"If I can have just a few more minutes of your time, we can get on with the meal," Cadin said.

Everyone turned to give Cadin their full attention. "I have some good news I want to share with you all." She nodded at Lexie who pulled the keys from her pocket and laid them on the table.

"What are those for?" Sister Frances asked.

"They are the keys to Miss Betty's home," Cadin said.

Miss Betty looked at her, confusion written all over her face. "I don't understand. How did you get the keys to my home?"

"I got them from the bank when I bought your home back today," Cadin said.

"You did what?" Sister Frances said.

"I bought the house back from the bank, but there are some special circumstances with this deal. Are you ready to hear them?" she asked Miss Betty, who was already crying.

She nodded her head. "Yes, thank you, Cadin."

"I bought the house in the name of the Missy Foundation. She's the woman I told you about the other night, so the house isn't actually in your name for tax purposes, but the house is yours." Cadin took a breath. "As I said I do have a couple of requirements. First, I want Terri and Lexie to move in with you on a temporary basis to give them a home. No offense, Sister Frances but Lexie needs her own room and the opportunity a stable home can give her."

"No offense. I agree with you completely," Sister Frances said.

"I would love to have them live with me," Miss Betty said.

"That is not a permanent solution, but it's a start. Terri will pay you one hundred dollars each week. Half of that you will put in a savings account for them and when they are ready to move into a place of their own, they will have startup money. The other half, you use as you see fit. Your only expenses will be the utilities. The foundation will pay any taxes and insurance on the property."

"Oh my good gracious," Miss Betty said. "I can't believe you have done this."

"Missy would have wanted this, so I think it's a perfect arrangement. Once Terri and Lexie move on to a place of their own, if you feel comfortable enough to help another woman out, please do."

Sister Frances was beaming with a smile.

"Tomorrow, Lexie and I will start cleaning up the garden for you, and Terri has agreed to help with cleaning the interior. I figure if we work together we can move your furniture and personal stuff back into the house Sunday or Monday, if we can rent a moving truck."

"I can ask the men from the church to move my stuff back in after church on Sunday," Miss Betty said. "I only have one bed though, so we'll have to find beds for Terri and Lexie."

"I will take care of that. If there is anything else you need to set up the home, let me know. Does this all sound acceptable to you?" she asked Miss Betty.

"Oh yes, Cadin, you have made my dreams come true."

"I think we can all work together and get the house cleaned and ready to go tomorrow," Sister Frances said.

"Lexie and I went inside this afternoon and it's not bad. Needs a good cleaning, but otherwise it's in good shape," Cadin said.

Miss Betty stood and walked over to Cadin and hugged her. "I can't thank you enough."

"You already have, Miss Betty, by showing me your kindness. Now ladies are we ready to eat?" she asked.


The conversation around the table buzzed with excitement, as they discussed plans to clean the house and grounds. Miss Betty's eyes remained full of tears of joy, and each time she looked at Cadin she smiled brightly, her heart filled with love and renewed hope.

# Chapter Four

The group spent the next two days preparing Miss Betty's home for occupation and by the end of Friday, they were satisfied with the results.

Cadin and Lexie worked hard to reclaim the garden plot and were surprised to find several of the plants bearing vegetables. They picked what they could and trimmed the weeds and vines back from the plants. They had created a huge pile of trimmings that one of Miss Betty's church friends would come to haul off for her.

When Miss Betty called an end to the workday, Lexie and Cadin climbed into Terri's car for the short ride home. "You two got a lot done today," Terri said.

"Yeah we did, but there's one more thing I want to do with the garden," Cadin said.

"What's that?" Terri asked.

"I want to rig up an irrigation system so Miss Betty just needs to turn on the faucet to water the whole garden at once."

"How long will that take?" Terri asked.

"Several hours once I get the hoses and sprinklers from the store," Cadin said.

"Why don't you see if you can borrow a car tomorrow and get the supplies and take them to the house? I go in late on Sunday, so Lexie and I can both help on Sunday morning," Terri said.

"You want to go shopping with me tomorrow?" Cadin asked Lexie.

Terri chuckled. "Do you really even have to ask?"

"I sure do," Lexie said.

†

After showering and dressing in clean clothes, Terri went to the kitchen to see if she could offer Sister Frances any help. Cadin and Lexie stretched out on their beds to relax.

"Will you help me with something tomorrow?" Lexie asked her.

"Sure, what do you need?"

"Mommy's birthday is Monday, so I'd like to use the money Sister Frances paid me to buy her a nice present."

Cadin smiled. "Is there anything in particular you have in mind?"

Lexie rolled onto her stomach and propped her head on her pillow. "There's a little jewelry shop on the square and there is a bracelet that Mommy likes in the front window. I'd like to see how much it costs," she said with a grin.

Cadin knew no matter what, Lexie would leave that store tomorrow with that bracelet and a smile came to her face. "Let's get up early then and get the supplies bought and delivered; then we can go to the jewelry store."

"Thanks," Lexie said. "Mommy never gets anything for her birthday."

"Why don't we see if Miss Betty will help you make a birthday cake too?"

"Do you think she would?"

"I bet she would love to."

"When do you think we will move into the house?"

Cadin looked at Lexie. "I think the plan is to be there Monday if everything gets moved Sunday."

"It would be nice to have a party in our new home."

"Yes, it would. Why don't you talk to Miss Betty tomorrow morning and see what you can get planned."

"I will," Lexie said. She grew quiet. Cadin knew Lexie wanted to ask something else, but she waited for the question to come.

"Will you be leaving us soon?" Lexie asked after a few minutes passed.

"Probably next week, I think I've done what I was sent here to do," Cadin answered.

"Will I ever see you again?" she asked, tears pooling in her eyes.

"Yes, you most definitely will, but I can't tell you when," Cadin assured her.

"I love working with you," Lexie said.

"It's been a lot of fun, hasn't it."

Lexie nodded as she wiped a tear from her cheek.

"I will be calling to check on you," Cadin said. "Soon you will be starting school and making all kinds of new friends."

"I know, but I'll be missing you."

Cadin felt a lump form in her throat. She hadn't anticipated how hard saying goodbye would be for her. "I'll miss you too, but there are still things I have to do before I go back home."

"Where will you go next?"

"I'm not sure yet, maybe you can help me with that?"

"How can I do that?" Lexie asked.

"For starters, run over to the house and ask Sister Frances for a roll of tape," Cadin said.

"I'll be right back." Lexie raced from the room.

✝

Cadin pulled out her duffel and dug through it until she found her road map and the container that held her lucky dart. She was unfolding the map when Lexie returned with a tape dispenser. "Tear me off a small piece of tape, please."

Lexie handed a small piece to Cadin who taped one top corner of the map to the wall. "I need one more piece, please."

Cadin taped the other corner and then opened the dart case. "This is the fun part," she said as she moved to the end of her bed. "Step back, in case my shot is wild," she teased.

Lexie moved to stand behind her.

She closed her eyes and took a deep breath. When she opened her eyes, she threw the dart at the map. "Let's go see where it landed."

Lexie rushed to the head of the bed. Her face screwed up as she looked at where the dart had landed.

"Bogalusa, Louisiana," Cadin said.

"That's how you decide for real?" Lexie said.

"Yes, you see this little hole here?" she said, pointing to the small hole next to Greensboro on the map. "That's how I got here."

Lexie cocked her head to the side as she looked at Cadin. "I'm so glad you came here."

"So am I," she admitted. "I've enjoyed being here." She pulled the dart from the wall, and placed it in the case and removed the map from the wall. "Now that that's settled, are you ready to eat?"

"Yes ma'am," Lexie said.

"Can you take the tape back to Sister Frances? I'll put my stuff away and be right there."

"Sure can, Cadin," she said and left the room.

She watched Lexie rush off and smiled. "Bogalusa, here I come," she said and tucked the map and dart case back into her duffel.

✝

The next morning she and Lexie took Miss Betty's car to the local hardware store and bought the supplies she needed for the irrigation system. They then dropped them off at the garden and rode back into town. Lexie pointed out the jewelry store and Cadin found a parking spot.

As they walked up to the store window, Lexie frowned. "I don't see the bracelet," she said.

"Maybe they just changed out the display. Let's go inside and see if it's still for sale," she said.

"Good morning," an elderly man said from behind the counter as they stepped through the door. "What can I do for you ladies this morning?"

"Tell him what you are looking for, Lexie."

"My mommy likes the bracelet you had in the front window and I wanted to buy it for her birthday, but I don't see it in the window anymore."

"Let's see. I just changed out the window this week and I put the bracelet back in the case over here," he said as he led them toward a large display case.

"Do you see the one she liked in here?" he asked.

Lexie moved closer to peer into the front of the case. She looked them over and then her eyes lit up when she spotted the one she was looking for. "That's it," she said. "The one with the green stone."

Cadin looked down at a gold and emerald bracelet. She watched as the man pulled the bracelet out of the case and handed it to her. "Is this the one?"

"Yes sir, that's the one," Lexie said. "Isn't it pretty, Cadin?"

Cadin bent down to examine the bracelet and saw the two-hundred-dollar price tag dangling from the clasp. "It's perfect for your mom," she said.

"How much is it?" Lexie asked.

The man smiled at her and asked, "How much do you have?"

Lexie started digging into her pocket to pull out her money. Cadin held up a credit card to show the man, and held up two fingers and then formed a zero with her index finger and thumb to tell the man to only take twenty dollars from Lexie.

The man smiled and nodded his understanding.

"I have this much," Lexie said, straining to place her money on the counter. "Is it enough?"

The man looked over her hard-earned cash, and selected a twenty-dollar bill. "This is just fine," he said. "Would you like it gift wrapped?" he asked.

"That would be great," she answered.

"You two look around and I'll get this wrapped for you," he said, taking Cadin's credit card.

They moved from case to case looking at the variety of jewelry. Cadin's eyes fell on a gold chain with a small Saint Christopher charm. "Would you wear a necklace if I bought you one?" she asked.

"Yes, I'd love one," Lexie said.

Cadin pointed out the charm she was looking at. "Saint Christopher is the patron Saint of Travelers. He watches over people to keep them safe. He can protect you after I'm gone," she said.

"It's beautiful," she said.

"We'll take this necklace too," Cadin said, much to the shopkeeper's delight.

"Would you like it wrapped?"

"No, I think she can wear this one out," she said with a wink.

The man took the necklace from the case, removed the price tag, and handed it to her. "Here you are," he said.

She knelt down in front of Lexie and placed the necklace around her neck. "There, just perfect for you."

Lexie reached forward, wrapped her arms around Cadin's neck, and kissed her cheek. "Thanks Cadin," she said.

"You're very welcome," she said and signed the credit card slip.

"Here's your present. I hope your mommy likes it," he said.

"Thanks," she said as she cradled the small box in her tiny hands.

"Thank you for the business," he said to Cadin.

"You're welcome," she said as they walked to the door.

On their way back to the car, she asked, "You still need to talk to Miss Betty this morning, don't you?"

"Yes, I do. I thought I'd do that when we get back," Lexie said

†

Lexie barreled into the sleeping quarters just as Cadin was drifting off for a nap.

"Everyone is ready to go to the dove hunt," Lexie rattled excitedly.

"I guess I had better get a move on then," Cadin said as she sat up and slipped her feet into her boots.

Cadin stood and stretched, then followed Lexie out into the midday sun. They walked over to the car where Sister Frances and Miss Betty were waiting.

"I hope you can wait another thirty minutes or so for some lunch," Sister Frances said. "We'll have lunch at the hunt."

"That's good for me," Cadin said as she slipped behind the wheel and started the car.

As Cadin approached a stoplight, Sister Frances said, "Cadin, pull into that liquor store on the left."

Cadin's foot slammed into the brake and the car screeched to a halt. "Wh...what did you say?" she asked with a stutter.

"The liquor store, just ahead on the left, will you stop in there?" she repeated.

"But, but, Sister Frances, you...you're a nun," Cadin said in total shock.

Sister Frances and Miss Betty burst out laughing in the backseat. Cadin and Lexie turned to look at them. The blaring of a horn from the car behind her brought her attention back to the stoplight, and she drove through the intersection, pulled into the small liquor store lot and parked the car. She turned in her seat and looked at Sister Frances for an explanation.

Tears rolled down the women's cheeks as they struggled to regain their composure. Cadin's shocked look threatened to send them into another round of laughter. "What is going on here?" she asked.

"You really think Sister Frances is a nun?" Miss Betty said, elbowing her friend.

"Well yes, the Sister part has me thinking she's a nun," Cadin answered.

"Dear child, I'm not even Catholic," Sister Frances said, still chuckling.

Cadin's face revealed she was still confused.

"Sister is just a term of respect," Miss Betty explained to a perplexed Cadin.

"I never thought of that. I just assumed with the shelter and all that you were a nun on a mission."

Sister Frances chuckled. "I am on a mission and right now, I wish you'd go inside, buy a bottle of Gentleman Jack for Miss Betty and me, and get whatever you'd like to drink today," she said as she handed Cadin a fifty-dollar bill.

Cadin shook her head as she emerged from the car and walked into the liquor store. "I sure missed that one," she mumbled to herself. She picked up a fifth of Sister Frances's requested liquor and since she was responsible for driving everyone home later, she settled for a six-pack of Corona. She carried her items to the counter.

"It must be dove hunt time," the young clerk said. "That's the only time I've ever seen Sister Frances drink," she added.

"Yes, we are headed there now," she replied.

"Have a great time," she said as she placed her purchases in a bag.

"We will," Cadin answered, taking the change and returning to the car.

She opened the back door and handed the bag to Miss Betty. Climbing back behind the wheel, she looked into the rearview mirror asking, "Are there any more stops?"

"Nope, let's go hunting," Sister Frances said with a grin from ear to ear.

†

Cadin turned off the highway onto a narrow tree-lined lane, and when she crested a hill, her eyes fell upon a field filled with a variety of vehicles from beat-up trucks to shiny sports cars. "I take it we have arrived?"

"Yes, we have," Miss Betty said with excitement.

Women of all ages, sizes, and color filled the yard. A dozen or more young girls were playing a game at the bottom of another hill, which caught Lexie's attention.

"Go ahead and introduce yourself," Miss Betty said.

Lexie looked up at Cadin who nodded and said, "Have fun."

"I will," Lexie said and took off at a run.

Miss Betty led her over to a group of women surrounding a cooker and introduced her to JC, the homeowner and organizer of the hunt.

"Welcome," JC said. "I hope you will make yourself at home here."

"Thanks. I have no idea what you're cooking, but it smells great."

"We're working on smoking a couple of pork shoulders here, but there's some beef brisket for sandwiches inside if you're hungry. Miss Betty, will you show Cadin around and introduce her?" JC asked.

"It will be my pleasure," Miss Betty said as she took Cadin's arm and introduced her to several groups of women before taking her inside. The women inside preparing sandwich plates were of an older crowd, the eldest, a sprite woman in her eighties, introduced herself as JC's grandma, Sue.

"Can I get you girls a plate of food?" she asked.

"Make it three please," Miss Betty said. "Sister Frances is out chatting with JC."

"It's good to see you ladies," Sue said. "There are so many of you I don't get to see but one time a year," she said as she poured chips onto three plates filled with steaming sandwiches.

"I know, we really should get together more often," Miss Betty said. "Time just seems to slip away."

"A whole lot faster for some of us," Sue said with a wink. "Can I get you something to drink?"

"I think Sister Frances is working on that," Miss Betty said as she accepted two plates. Sue handed Cadin a plate.

"Thanks," Cadin said and followed Miss Betty back outside. Every television inside and out was tuned to one football game or another as they left the house.

Women in their twenties covered the deck as they enthusiastically cheered for a favored home team. "I think we'll pass on this crowd for a while," Miss Betty said as she led Cadin to several picnic tables strategically placed safely away from the rowdy football crowd. "I think it's safe to eat here."

"Here they are," Sister Frances said as she and another woman arrived and took seats.

Sister Frances was speaking with an attractive, dark-haired woman and when Cadin turned to face the newcomer, the deep green of her eyes threatened to take her breath away. Cadin couldn't tear her gaze away for several long seconds, until she realized Sister Frances was speaking.

"Renee, this is Cadin Michaels," Sister Frances said. "She's a lawyer up your way."

"Hello," Cadin said. "Don't hold the whole lawyer thing against me."

"Oh, I won't," the woman said with a brilliant smile.

"Cadin, this is Dr. Renee Allen."

"Pleasure to meet you," she said.

"Likewise," Renee answered.

"I swapped out for a cold Corona for you," Sister Frances said.

"Thanks," Cadin said, finally tearing her eyes away from Renee.

"Have you already eaten, Renee?" Miss Betty asked.

"Yes, I think I was first in line. I had to smell it cooking all night last night."

"You came over last night?" Sister Frances asked.

"Yes, I came in about three. JC and some of the others were getting the brisket ready to cook."

"Renee is JC's baby sister," Miss Betty explained. "She's a vet and lives in Stone Mountain."

"Not far from me then," Cadin said.

"What brings you to Greensboro from the big city?" Renee asked.

"I'm taking a sabbatical from work to travel for a while," Cadin answered. Her eyes moved over to the group of girls playing and smiled when she saw Lexie fitting in comfortably.

Renee followed her gaze. "Is the little one you arrived with yours?"

Cadin smiled at the thought. "No, but I'd be proud to have a daughter like Lexie."

"She and her mom have been staying with me for a short time," Sister Frances chimed in.

Lexie looked up to see them watching the group, smiled and waved to them. Cadin waved back. "She's a great kid."

"She also thinks highly of you," Miss Betty replied.

"Those two have knocked out the harvesting of my pecans in just a few short days," Sister Frances added, nodding toward Cadin.

"She may be young, but she's a slave driver," Cadin teased.

Cadin watched Lexie and the others play for several more minutes before turning back to her meal. "This meat is really good," she said with a moan.

Renee chuckled. "It should be, JC got up at four this morning to put it on the smoker."

"I hope she went back to bed," Miss Betty said.

"No, we took the opportunity to drink coffee and catch up on life. It's been several months since JC and I had a long talk."

Miss Betty nodded her understanding. "How's she doing after the breakup?"

"She was devastated at first, but she's come to understand she's much better off without Brenda draining her energy and bank account. JC had me worried for a while though."

"I saw her in town a few months ago and she'd lost a bunch of weight. I asked her to drop by for dinner some night, but I knew she wasn't ready to talk about what happened. I'm glad she's looking better now," Sister Frances remarked.

Renee smirked. "Mama threatened to move in with her if she didn't start eating."

"I love your mama, but Julia is a force to be reckoned with," Sister Frances said. "I'm glad her tactics worked though. JC is a good woman."

Cadin continued to eat as the others talked, her attention torn between listening to them and watching Lexie playing with a group of girls. One of them had found a playground ball and they were embroiled in a serious game of kickball. She watched as Lexie kicked the ball over a fielder's head and ran to the makeshift base. A grin spread across her face as her team clapped for her performance.

"That was quite a kick," Renee said.

"Yes, it was. She's pretty fast for her size too."

"I'm ready for another drink," Sister Frances announced. "May we bring you two fresh beers?"

"Yes, that would be great," Cadin answered.

Miss Betty picked up on Sister Frances's lead and followed her over to the makeshift bar to help pour the drinks.

"Those two are quite the pair," Renee said as she watched them at the bar.

"They are amazing women," Cadin stated. "I've enjoyed getting to know them."

Renee smiled at her. "You must be something special too for Sister Frances to invite you to the hunt. Not just anyone is welcome."

Cadin smiled, remembering her shock earlier. "You know until about an hour ago I thought she was a nun."

Laughing, Renee said, "You're probably not the first to be fooled by her title. She's been Sister Frances for as long as I've known her."

"Did you grow up here?"

"Born and raised in Greensboro. I moved to Stone Mountain after college when a classmate invited me to start a practice with him."

"That's quite a change from a laid-back little country town," Cadin noted.

Renee grinned. "Yeah it is, but close enough I can come home when I need some fresh country air."

"That's cool."

"So, is Atlanta home for you?"

"Yeah, I've been there my entire life," Cadin answered.

"I've enjoyed living there, but I've spent so much time working I haven't seen much of the city."

Cadin easily took the bait offered. "I'd be glad to show you the sights sometime."

Renee smiled nervously. "That was a bit cheesy of me wasn't it?"

"It wasn't cheesy at all. I'd really like to share my hometown with you," Cadin said to put Renee at ease.

Renee reached into her bag, pulled out a business card and jotted her cell phone number on the back before handing it to Cadin. "Give me a call when you return home."

"I will," she said, returning her smile as she tucked the card into her wallet.

Miss Betty and Sister Frances returned with cold beers and took their seats. "We couldn't have asked for a better day."

"No, the weather's turned out perfect," Cadin said as a burst of cheering sounded from the deck.

"'Bama must have scored," Renee said. "I'm going to check on JC. Do you ladies need anything?"

"No, I think we are good for now," Miss Betty answered.

†

Lexie took a break from the game and rushed over to the table to sit beside Cadin and drink some water.

"Are you having fun?"

Her smile beamed as Lexie placed her bottle on the table. "I think I will be in the same grade with two of the girls I'm playing with, but they're all very nice."

"Are you hungry?" Miss Betty asked.

"Yes, ma'am, a little," she answered.

"Let me go get you a plate while you finish your game then."

"Thanks Miss Betty," Lexie said and rushed back to her new friends.

"I don't think we need to worry about her fitting in," Sister Frances told Cadin.

"Will you keep in touch and let me know if she needs anything after I leave?"

"You know I will," she answered. "Are you leaving us soon?"

Cadin turned to look at her. "I was thinking early next week, after they get settled in at Miss Betty's."

Sister Frances smiled warmly. "I hope you know you're welcome to return anytime you want."

Cadin returned her smile. "I appreciate that. I've really enjoyed being here."

"We've enjoyed having you with us. You've done so much for all of us."

"I've felt very at home here and you're doing so much for the women who need your help."

She smiled at Cadin. "Like you, I'm doing what my heart tells me is right."

†

Cadin spent the next several hours milling among the crowd, talking to a variety of women. When she made her way back into the kitchen for some tea, she was welcomed by a circle of older women sitting in the den. She walked into the kitchen and took a cup of tea from Sue as the ladies continued talking.

"It's sad we are short two of our regulars this year," Sue told her.

"Why, what happened that they couldn't make it?"

"Elverna Ledbetter passed on a few short months ago at the ripe old age of seventy-four," Sue said and then frowned before she spoke again. "Alice Turner was just twenty-six when she died this year in an automobile accident. She left behind two small children and a husband."

"It's always hard when someone young is taken in their prime," Cadin said, her words striking close to home.

"I hope you don't mind, but Sister Frances told us what you've done for Miss Betty, and that young woman and her child. We as a community can't thank you enough for stepping in on her behalf."

"No one should be treated like that, especially someone as dear as Miss Betty. I'm honored to be able to help them out."

"We have been blessed by you and I hope you will consider returning next year for our little party."

Cadin chuckled. "I'd love that. It's heartwarming to see such great friends, and a community of women, bonding like you do here."

"You're a part of that community now and will be welcome any time you choose to join us."

"Thanks, that means a great deal to me."

Terri walked into the kitchen, having arrived after work. "I hear this is the place to get some great food," she said.

Sue beamed with joy at Terri's praise. "Sue, this is Terri Foster, Lexie's mom," Cadin introduced them.

"Welcome Terri, and I must say that daughter of yours is the spitting image of her mama."

"One heck of a kickball player too," Cadin added. "She's already made several new friends."

"I'm so pleased to hear that," Terri said. "She's been dying to meet some girls her age."

Sue handed her a plate of food. "May I get you something else, Cadin?"

"Thanks, Sue, but I'm holding out for some of that pork shoulder later," she answered.

"I'll be sure to make you a big plate then," Sue said with a wink.

"Fantastic," Cadin said. "Let me take you out to the picnic tables. I think the game is still in full tilt."

†

As they passed the deck, Renee looked up from the conversation she was having and caught Cadin's eye and smiled.

Cadin felt a soft flush rise to her cheeks when she realized Renee had caught her staring. She smiled back and continued to walk with Terri to the picnic tables.

Lexie saw them approach and came rushing to the table, breathless with excitement. "Hey Mommy, I'm having so much fun," she said.

"So I see, and I hear you are an awesome kickball player."

"Our team is winning," she said and took a drink of her water.

A roar from the deck caught their attention as one of the football teams scored a touchdown, much to the crowd's delight. She watched Renee get pulled into a group hug and smiled. Renee had probably grown up with most of the women occupying the deck and it was good to see how much they were enjoying themselves.

"May I get you an adult beverage?" Sister Frances asked.

"What are you having?"

"Jack and Coke," she answered.

"Oh, goodness, nothing that strong, I'm driving home later."

"I have a few Coronas left if you'd rather have one of those," Cadin said.

"That would be good," she said.

Cadin made a move to stand and Sister Frances said, "Sit tight, I'll get it. Do you want another?"

"No, I think I'll stick to tea for now," she answered.

†

As the sun faded, so did the energy of the young girls who had played together all day, Lexie among them. She climbed up the hill on tired legs and climbed onto the bench beside her mother.

"Did you have fun today?" she asked her daughter.

"Yes, I did, Mommy, but I'm hungry and tired now."

"I bet we can get you a plate and then you and I can go home, honey," Terri answered.

"I think we should all grab a plate," Miss Betty said.

They were about to rise when Renee approached carrying two plates. "Grandma fixed you a plate," she said as she placed the two plates on the table.

"We were just getting ready to get some food," Cadin said.

"All you need is something to drink, unless this plate isn't big enough for you," she teased.

"That plate is humongous. What would you like to drink?"

"I'll take some tea if that's where you're headed."

Cadin smiled. "That's exactly where I'm going. Be right back."

"Do you want me to sneak a peek at the dessert table for you?" Sister Frances asked.

Cadin chuckled. "I already have, but you can bring me a bowl of banana pudding if you have a free hand."

"No problem," she said and walked with the others to the kitchen.

†

Cadin returned carrying two glasses of tea and sat across from Renee. "This all looks so good I don't know where to start."

"Definitely with the shoulder, it will almost melt in your mouth. I've been trying for years to get JC's sauce recipe, but she won't share it even with her sister."

Cadin took a bite and moaned. "I can see why you want it, this is fabulous." Cadin looked down at the mound of food on her plate. "Your grandma must have thought I was starving."

"She never wants anyone to go away hungry."

"I may need a wheelbarrow if I manage to eat all this."

"Well, just don't forget you have some of my banana pudding coming, so save some room."

"You made that banana pudding?"

"I've been making it every year for the hunt for twenty years now," Renee said.

"That's amazing, that you all have been meeting for so long."

"It was Gran's idea. Our first crowd was about a dozen women, and you see what it's grown into."

"So does everyone have a particular item they are responsible for?"

"Several of us do. JC, of course, is the grill master and prepares all the meats. Others bring a variety of salads, vegetables, and desserts." Renee smirked. "The young ones, as Gran calls them, bring the drinks and paper goods, which usually accounts for a keg or two of beer, cases of sodas, all the plates, napkins, and utensils."

"Sounds like y'all have this down to a science."

"If someone can't make it, for some reason or another, then another woman takes up the slack. Miss

Elverna used to make the best potato salad, but now that she's passed on Mama makes it instead."

"I can't imagine any tasting better than this," Cadin said. "It's all too good to be true, and on one plate to boot."

"It's quite the affair," Renee said. "JC has cots set up in her work shed for the deck hands as she calls them." Renee nodded to the crowd on the deck. "They're the football crowd. They will drain the kegs and pass out in stages down in the shed. JC will feed them a good breakfast in the morning and then they'll get to work cleaning up from the party."

"Amazing," Cadin said, truly impressed.

"The early teens and younger children will head home after dinner with the older women and then the partying begins in earnest."

"It gets wilder?"

"Oh, you haven't seen anything yet." Renee chuckled. "The closer the games are on television, the rowdier the crowd. Lord help us all if a team from Alabama loses, especially to LSU or Georgia."

"They take their football serious do they?"

"It's almost like a religion," Renee said with a smirk.

†

When the others returned carrying plates of food, Cadin eyed the bowl of banana pudding. She was barely three quarters done with her meal when she couldn't hold back any longer. "I have to have that pudding right now," she finally announced.

Sister Frances handed her the bowl. "Eat until your heart's content," she said.

"I'm planning on it," she said and placed a spoonful in her mouth. "Oh, my goodness, this is good," she said between bites. "You really made this?"

"Like I said, I've made the banana pudding for almost twenty years," Renee reminded her.

"I'd say you've got it down to an art then. I could make a meal of this."

Curious to see what the fuss was about, Lexie slipped her spoon into the creamy dessert and swiped a bite.

"Hey, no stealing," Cadin said with a grin.

"This is yummy," Lexie said. "May I have some, Mommy?"

"After you finish your dinner," Terri said and then stood up.

"Where are you going?" Cadin asked.

"Back to the kitchen to get a bowl for Lexie before it all disappears," she answered.

"Get two and Betty and I will split one," Sister Frances said.

Terri looked at Renee, who shook her head. "Trust me I ate plenty while I was making it, you go right ahead."

✝

After dessert, they all declared they couldn't eat another bite. Lexie climbed up into Terri's lap and promptly fell asleep. "I guess I should take her home," Terri said when the child began softly snoring.

Cadin smiled at the sleeping girl. "She played hard today and made some new friends."

"I'm so thankful you invited us," Terri told Sister Frances.

"I'm glad you got to come. You're a part of our family now."

Cadin could see tears welling in Terri's eyes. "Do you want me to carry her up to the car for you?"

"Thanks, but I'm used to carrying her. You can walk up with me though if you'd like."

"You two go ahead and we'll clean up these dishes while you're gone," Miss Betty said.

"I'll be right back then," Cadin said.

"She really did have fun today," Terri said as they walked to the car.

"This is a good bunch of women to be associated with," Cadin said. "I bet every one of them would give you the shirt off their backs if you needed it."

Terri looked up at Cadin when they reached the car and the light of the moon sparkled in her eyes. "You know, for the first time in forever, I feel like I've found home."

"You are home," Cadin said. She held the door open for Terri to place Lexie across the backseat. "Be careful and I will see you later."

Terri hugged Cadin close. "Thank you for everything. Somehow I don't think things would have turned out like they have if you hadn't arrived."

"Sure they would have. Maybe I just sped them up a bit," Cadin said and kissed the top of Terri's head. Terri climbed into the car and Cadin closed the door behind her.

When she returned to the table, Miss Betty and Sister Frances were mixing themselves a drink. "One more and then I think we'll be ready to head home if you are," Miss Betty said. "You have a Corona left," she said, handing the icy beer to Cadin.

"Do you have any idea when you will be headed back to Atlanta?" Renee asked.

"No, not as of yet, but I'd like to call you while I'm gone."

"I would like that too," she said as the first of a string of fireworks exploded in the night sky.

## Chapter Five

Sunday morning arrived all too soon for Cadin's taste. She woke with the bitter aftertaste of beer in her mouth and went straight to the bathroom to brush her teeth. She had left the party within an hour of Terri and Lexie, but it felt like she had just drifted off to sleep when Roscoe started crowing. She rinsed her face with cold water, then dressed before going to the house for coffee.

"Good morning," Lexie said cheerfully when she saw Cadin come through the door.

"Good morning. Are those pancakes I smell cooking?"

"Yes, Mommy is cooking this morning."

"Hey Cadin, you look like you could use some coffee," Terri said as she poured a cup.

"At least a pot," Cadin said with a grin as Miss Betty and Sister Frances entered at the same time.

"Better make that a couple pots," Sister Frances said.

Terri poured them all cups and carried them to the table. "Who else besides my little one wants pancakes?"

"I'll take a short stack," Cadin said.

"I think I'll stick to coffee for now," Sister Frances said.

"Me too," moaned Miss Betty. "I'm glad the hunt is only once a year." She took a sip of the strong coffee.

"I wish it was every weekend," Lexie said.

"Don't worry, you'll have plenty of friends. Brittany, one of the girls you were playing with, only lives a block away from our home," Miss Betty told her.

"Cool," she answered and walked into the kitchen to take a plate of pancakes from her mom. "Are we still going to work on the garden this morning, Cadin?"

"Yes, ma'am, we are. With your mom's help we should finish in no time."

"A group of men from the church are coming by after lunch, and with their trucks we should get everything moved back to the house today," Miss Betty told them. "I'm so excited to be home again."

"Two new beds and some other furniture will be delivered tomorrow," Cadin said. "That should have you all set."

"Thank you again for everything," Miss Betty said with tears threatening to fall.

"You are very welcome and I know these two will be good company for you," Cadin said as Terri brought her a plate of pancakes.

"Yes, we will," she answered.

"I'll admit, I'm going to miss your help in the kitchen once you're gone," Sister Frances said.

"The other women will pitch in to help you out until another poor soul comes along," Miss Betty said. "If you get in a bind and need my help though, remember I'm just a call away."

"I will," she answered.

The conversation around the table that morning was filled with excitement as the time drew near for them to move home. Only Cadin felt the tug of sadness as she realized it would soon be time to move on to her next adventure. She had decided to leave on Tuesday, after the move was done. She smiled as she listened to the friendly banter around the table and knew she would miss the dear friends she had grown to love.

†

Cadin rode behind Terri and Lexie to Miss Betty's house and their new home. With the added help from Terri, the irrigation project was finished quickly. They were sitting on the wooden swing enjoying the late morning when Sister Frances pulled up in her car. Terri looked at her watch, fearing she was running late for work, but saw that it was just eleven.

"You're earlier than planned," Cadin said as Sister Frances approached.

"The pastor was so excited about the news of Miss Betty going home, he cut his sermon short so the men could get her moved in," she answered. "The first truck is only minutes behind me."

"I guess we had better get the house opened up then. Did you bring your key?" Cadin asked Lexie.

"Are you kidding, she's had it in her pocket since the moment you gave her a copy," Terri said.

"We'll let you do the honors then. Run and open the front and back doors for the movers," Cadin said.

Lexie flew off the swing and ran to the back door. She unlocked the door and carefully propped it open before dashing through the house to repeat the process with the front door. Slightly winded when she returned, she climbed back in the swing. "All set." She grinned.

When the trucks started rolling in the house began to take shape as a home. Terri helped Miss Betty unpack dishes in the kitchen while Lexie and Cadin carried in smaller boxes. The men from the church did the heavy lifting and assembled Miss Betty's bed before heading for home. When Terri left to get ready for work, the living room was a mound of boxes.

"I really hate to leave, but I'll be late for work if I don't go soon."

"No worries, we will unpack what we can tonight and start on it again tomorrow," Miss Betty said. "It's just good to be home."

"I will see you all later tonight then."

"Have a great day at work, Mommy," Lexie said as she walked her to the door.

"I love you, baby," she said.

"I love you too, Mommy."

†

Later that afternoon, Cadin ordered pizza delivered, and they added the empty boxes to the growing pile on the front porch. They had made a sizeable dent in the mound of boxes, but there was still plenty work to be completed. As the afternoon burned away, Miss Betty announced, "I think we have done enough for one day. I thank you all for your help."

Cadin and Lexie locked the doors after taking the last of the empty boxes to the porch. "May I ride home with you?" Lexie asked.

"Not this time, kiddo. You still have a cake to bake and I have an errand to run. Ride back with Miss Betty and I will see you soon."

Cadin rode to the department store on the edge of town where she bought a gift card. Cadin had purchased beds, but never gave thought to linens. With a gift card Terri could buy the linens of their choosing. As an afterthought, Cadin walked into the electronics department and bought two simple point-and-shoot digital cameras, one for her and one for Lexie. She would take pictures before she left to remind her of all the wonderful memories she had shared with her new friends and would show Lexie how to use the camera to make memories of her own.

†

Miss Betty and Lexie were putting the finishing touches to the birthday cake when Cadin arrived. "That turned out really well," she commented.

"Miss Betty will take it to the house in the morning so we can have a party for Mommy, when she gets home from work," Lexie told her.

"Do you have a grill, Miss Betty?"

"Yes, there's one in the shed. Are you planning a dinner?"

Cadin looked at Lexie. "I thought it might be nice to have a cookout, some burgers, and hot dogs. What do you think, Lexie?"

"That would be awesome."

"I will make some baked beans and we can cook some french fries," Sister Frances added.

Cadin pulled out her wallet and took out two twenty-dollar bills. "Will this cover the groceries?"

"With money left over," Sister Frances said. "I'll go first thing in the morning."

Cadin smiled at Lexie. "Are you done helping Miss Betty?"

Lexie looked up at Miss Betty who smiled and nodded to the young girl.

"Come then, we still have something to do," Cadin said, holding out her hand.

✝

Cadin removed the two cameras and handed one to Lexie. "I wanted to show you how to use this so you can take pictures tomorrow at your mom's party. After that, I want you to keep the camera so you can send me pictures from time to time of what you've been up to," she added.

"You mean this is mine?"

"All yours and I got one just like it for me. Are you ready to learn how to use it?"

Within the hour, Lexie had learned how to use the camera. Cadin was amazed how quickly Lexie learned and how good her first shots turned out. They snuck back into the kitchen and took shots of Miss Betty and Sister Frances as they shelled pecans.

"Those came out great. You didn't even cut off a head like I usually do," Cadin teased.

She sat with the women and joined in on the shelling as Lexie practiced with her camera. She would take several shots and then rush back to show Cadin.

"I do believe we will need to buy some photo albums soon," Miss Betty said as Lexie rushed outside to take more pictures.

She had just returned inside to show off her sunset pictures when Terri arrived home from work. "Mommy," Lexie yelled, "look what Cadin bought for me," she said, holding the camera up for her to see.

Terri smiled at Cadin. "You are spoiling her rotten."

"Yeah, I am," Cadin said. "It's selfish of me though, because I can see what she's been doing after I leave."

Terri frowned. "Are you planning to leave soon?"

"I'm going to start out Tuesday morning."

"That's only a day away. We are going to miss you."

A smile crossed Cadin's face. "I'm going to miss you all too, but I'll be back. That's a promise."

The room fell quiet for a few minutes until Cadin broke the silence. "Dang, I almost forgot," she said as she pulled the gift card from her pocket and handed it to Terri. "The beds for you and Lexie will be delivered and set up tomorrow, but I didn't think to get linens. Maybe you and Lexie can go and pick some out."

Terri took the card and noted the amount written on the back of the card. "That's a lot of linens."

"Get several sets, some towels, and other items you might need. I'd also suggest a couple of memory cards and some photo albums for our aspiring photographer," she said, nodding toward Lexie.

Terri looked at Lexie. "Do you want to get up early in the morning to go or would you like to go tonight?"

"Are you too tired to go tonight?"

"No, honey, I'm good. Just let me change clothes." Terri turned to Cadin. "Would you like to join us?"

"I think I'll stay and chat with Sister Frances and Miss Betty," Cadin said.

"We'll see you later then," Terri said. "Let's go, honey," she said and left the room.

✝

Miss Betty handed Cadin a basket of pecans. "Do you really have to leave so soon?"

"I think I've done what I came to do here," she answered.

"We can't thank you enough for all that you've done for us, but we will hate to see you leave."

Cadin cracked a nut. "It won't be easy to leave. I feel like I've made some great friends here."

"You have," Sister Frances agreed. "I have a feeling there will be many others on your journey before you make it home."

"None will be as special as this group," Cadin said. "You've made me feel like family."

"That's because you are family to us," Miss Betty said.

She looked up from the nut she was shelling. "Thank you for that, but you better stop before you make me cry."

Miss Betty chuckled. "All right, but remember sometimes it's good to cry."

"Your advice is noted," Cadin said and cracked another nut.

†

The conversation turned lighter as they shelled the nuts. When the door burst open and Lexie rushed back inside, she caught them all by surprise. She was carrying a bag nearly as big as she was. Terri followed closely behind her. "You should see what all we got," Lexie announced.

"I think we are about to get a show," Sister Frances said as Terri set the bags down and started placing the items on the table.

They made a big production of reviewing the purchases and Lexie's eyes were alight with excitement. "I can't wait to set up my room tomorrow."

"You will need a good night's sleep for that," Terri said. "Tell everyone goodnight and let's go."

"Yes, Mommy," Lexie answered then went around the table and gave them each a hug. "Are you coming too, Cadin?"

Cadin returned her smile. "Yes, I think I'll turn in too. Tomorrow will be a busy day for all of us. Goodnight ladies," she said and helped Terri carry the bags to Miss Betty's car.

†

By midmorning, the trucks had arrived and delivered the beds. When the driver had packed up the last of the boxes from the delivery and set up, Cadin, and Lexie went to work making the beds.

"Let's do Mommy's first," she said.

They worked together to place the linens on the bed and once the pillows were tucked into place Miss Betty called out, "Time for lunch, you two."

"On our way," Cadin called back.

Miss Betty had made fresh chicken salad. A plate of cheese, crackers, and fresh fruit sat in the middle of the kitchen table. They had just begun eating when Sister Frances arrived. "I'll be right back," Cadin said and went out to carry the bags of groceries for Sister Frances.

"Thanks for the help."

"Thanks for going shopping. That's never been one of my favorite activities."

Sister Frances smiled at her. "My pleasure."

"You arrived just in time to join us for lunch. We're having a light meal and a break from setting up house."

"How's it looking?"

"Pretty good. We have Terri's bed made and will work on Lexie's after lunch."

"This place is looking great," Sister Frances said as she looked around.

Cadin put the groceries in the refrigerator and stored the dry goods in the pantry before returning to the kitchen table.

"Grab a drink and come join us," Miss Betty said.

"Don't mind if I do," Sister Frances said as she walked into the kitchen. "What do you need my help with?"

"You can help me set up my bedroom when we finish lunch," Miss Betty said. "Cadin and Lexie will work on her room and by that time I would expect Terri will be on her way home and we can unpack her car."

"We don't have much," Lexie said.

"You have plenty to get you started. Once you're settled, you and your mom will start adding items you need," Cadin said. "I imagine you will need to do some clothes shopping soon to get ready for school."

"I can't wait for school to start."

"Next week will be here before you know it," Miss Betty said.

"Then we will blink and it will be Christmas," Sister Frances added.

Cadin chuckled. "Time does seem to fly by these days."

They went back to work after lunch and didn't break again until they heard Terri's car arrive. Cadin and Lexie went out to greet her.

"Happy birthday, Mommy!" Lexie said as she rushed over to hug and kiss her mother.

"Yes, happy birthday."

"Thanks you two. How are things coming along in the house?"

"Things are looking great. Lexie and I thought we'd help you unload the car and then you can relax for a little while. You must be tired after working."

"I was so excited about moving in today, the day flew by for me," Terri said.

"Let's get cracking then," Cadin said and opened the back door. Cadin handed several small bags to Lexie, lifting several of the larger bags, while Terri brought others inside.

"Those are Lexie's," Terri said and Cadin carried them into the room. After several trips, the car was unloaded and they began to unpack. "You two did a great job on the beds."

"Thanks," Cadin said. "Did you think to pick up clothes hangers last night?"

"Yes, I bought plenty. They are in those bags," she said, pointing to several large bags.

"We'll get her clothes put away and hung up, then help you if you'd like."

"That would be great," Terri answered and walked into her room.

✝

Once the clothes were properly stored, Cadin and Lexie went outside to set up the grill. The other women and kids from the shelter were starting to arrive and Miss Betty was shouting directions in the kitchen. Hamburgers molded into patties, onions and tomatoes were sliced, and lettuce washed to prepare for dinner. Cadin soaked the charcoal with lighter fluid, started the fire, and joined Lexie on the swing. "Welcome home," she said to the smiling child.

"Are you sure you can't stay longer, Cadin?"

"The sooner I get on my way, the sooner I can go home," she answered.

Lexie grinned. "This could be your home too."

She chuckled. "Nice try, kiddo, but I have to go back to Atlanta. I have a business to run and a home to care for there."

"I know," Lexie said with a frown.

"I'll be back and maybe you and your mom can come for a visit."

Lexie's head flew up. "I'd really like that."

"I'd like it too. When do you plan to give your mom her present?"

"After we eat, before we have cake."

"That sounds like the perfect time."

Cadin checked the coals. "I'm going to get the burgers."

"Wait for me and I'll help you," Lexie said as she jumped off the swing.

"Is everything set for your mom's surprise?"

"Yes, ma'am, the candles are on the cake already." Lexie and Miss Betty planned to light the candles and carry the cake to the table after everyone had finished dinner.

"Awesome," Cadin said and held the door open for Lexie.

†

When they returned outside, a car was pulling into the drive. Cadin smiled to see it was Renee carrying a large shopping bag. "Hello," she said as Renee walked up. "I thought you would already be on your way home."

"I heard there was a party going on so I decided to stay an extra day to help celebrate the homecoming. Do you mind if I crash your party?"

Cadin looked at Lexie who shook her head and then smiled up at Renee. "We don't mind at all. Why don't you take your bag inside and you can join us at the grill if you'd like."

"I'll be right back then," she said. Lexie ran ahead of her to open the door.

"Well, that's a nice surprise," Cadin said to herself. She hadn't expected to see Renee again until she returned home.

†

After she finished eating, Cadin took out her camera and snapped several shots of her extended family. She watched as Lexie and Miss Betty disappeared from the table into the kitchen. Several minutes later, Lexie burst out of the kitchen and shouted, "Happy Birthday, Mommy!"

Miss Betty followed behind her, carrying the cake, candles ablaze, as the group began singing "Happy Birthday." She placed the cake on the table in front of Terri and Lexie said, "Make a wish, Mommy."

Terri closed her eyes and leaned forward to blow out the candles to a chorus of cheers and clapping. Her eyes filled with tears when Lexie lifted a small gift box to her.

"Happy birthday, Mommy," she said and kissed her cheek.

Terri carefully removed the paper from the box as Lexie held her breath. When she opened the box to see the beautiful bracelet, she burst out in tears. "Thank you, honey," she said and leaned down to kiss her daughter. Then she looked up at Cadin. "Thank you for making this the best birthday ever."

"She used her harvesting money and picked it out all by herself. She said you had seen it and fell in love with the bracelet."

"I can't believe you remembered."

"I love you, Mommy, and wanted to get it for you."

"You did really, really well," Terri said and pulled her close. "Will you help me put it on?"

After a few tries, Lexie finally managed to fasten the bracelet. Her face glowed with pride when she looked up from her mother's wrist.

Terri opened the other gifts, and Renee handed Miss Betty a shopping card.

"JC and I wanted to give y'all this to stock up on grocery basics to get you started."

"Please send out thanks to JC. This will come in very handy," Miss Betty said.

✝

After the birthday celebration, Miss Betty said, "We have one more surprise tonight." She and Lexie went to a small table beside the door, reached inside her purse and handed a card to Lexie.

Lexie carried the card to Cadin and handed it to her, then kissed her cheek. "Thank you for giving us a home."

Cadin carefully opened the envelope and pulled out a card. Everyone from Sister Frances's had made a comment and signed the thank-you card. She read all of the comments as tears rolled down her cheeks and looked up to see everyone watching her. "Thanks to all of you," she said.

✝

After cleaning the kitchen, the women started to head for home. When Renee, Cadin, and Sister Frances were the last ones remaining, Lexie hugged Cadin. "Will you come by before you leave tomorrow?"

"You bet I will," Cadin answered.

"I'll cook breakfast if you'll eat with us," Miss Betty said.

"You've got a deal," Cadin said. "I'll see you all in the morning."

Lexie and Renee walked out to the bike with her. Cadin straddled the bike and turned back to her. "Enjoy sleeping in your own room tonight. I'll miss your snoring," she teased.

Lexie broke down and started crying.

Cadin climbed off the bike and knelt down to take her in her arms. "Please don't cry," she whispered.

"I'm going to miss you," Lexie said, gasping for breath.

"I will call to check on you and I will come back, so be strong for your mom and Miss Betty."

She wiped at her eyes and smiled at Cadin. "I'll try," she said.

"That's all I can ask," Cadin said and hugged her tight. "I'll see you in the morning."

"Goodnight, Cadin."

"Goodnight, Lexie. Sweet dreams," she said.

"You too," she said and turned to run back to the house.

Cadin watched until she went inside and turned to find Renee smiling at her.

"What?"

"I hope you realize that child loves you dearly."

"I do and the feeling's mutual. I'd love to have a child like her one day."

"Hopefully you will," Renee said. "Where are you off to next?"

"Bogalusa, Louisiana," she answered.

"Never heard of it, but I hope the town is ready for you," she teased.

"It can't be half as great as this one's been," Cadin said.

"You never know," Renee said. "Call me and let me know how things are going and when you think you'll be home. I'm looking forward to your guided tour of Atlanta."

Cadin chuckled. "I most certainly will."

Renee stepped forward to embrace her. "Stay safe and enjoy your journey. I'll be talking to you soon."

"I will and I promise to call once I'm settled."

"Goodnight Cadin."

"G'night ma'am," Cadin said and tipped an imaginary hat, making Renee smile.

She watched Renee climb into her car then mounted her bike to ride back to Sister Frances's home. Leaving was going to be much harder than she ever imagined.

The sleeping quarters felt empty without, Lexie, Terri, and Miss Betty. She pulled her duffel from under the bed and safely stored her gear. She kept out a clean outfit and then dressed for bed. She had just finished preparing for bed and climbed under the covers when she heard Sister Frances return home.

The following morning, Cadin showered, dressed, and packed the rest of her belongings into the duffel. She placed an envelope on the bed with Sister Frances's name written on the outside. Inside were two hundred-dollar bills to cover the rest of her stay. Cadin would leave it there for her, knowing full well Sister Frances would not accept it without an argument. Smiling, she carried the bag to her bike and secured it before going to the kitchen. The house lights were on and she walked in to find Sister Frances pouring a cup of coffee. She looked up when Cadin entered. "I hoped you would stop in to say goodbye."

"I couldn't leave without seeing you. Are you not going to Miss Betty's for breakfast?"

"I'd love to, but to be honest I can't stand to see Lexie's heart breaking when you leave. Last night was bad enough."

"She's a great kid."

"She loves you like a second mom."

"Yes, I know," Cadin answered with a deep sigh.

"Would you like some coffee?"

"I think I'd better pass and head on to Miss Betty's. I have a long ride ahead of me today."

Sister Frances had tears in her eyes. "Please keep in touch," she said as she hugged Cadin. "I can't thank you enough for all that you've done."

"It's nothing compared to what you have done for years," Cadin said. "I'll give you all a call in a couple days."

"Be safe then. I hope your heart finds the peace it seeks."

"Me too," Cadin said and hugged Sister Frances one last time then rushed from the room.

†

Cadin's heart was aching when she pulled into Miss Betty's yard and Lexie came rushing from the house. "Good morning, Cadin."

"Good morning. How was your room last night?"

"It was great," she said as she took Cadin's hand and they walked into the house.

"Good morning," Cadin said to Terri and Miss Betty. "You've got it smelling terrific in here."

"We thought we'd send you off with a full stomach," Miss Betty said as she placed a platter of bacon on the table.

The meal was fantastic and the time flew by too quickly. Terri stood and hugged Cadin. "I've got to go to work. Thanks again for everything."

"My pleasure," Cadin said.

Terri hugged Lexie, who had become quiet during the meal. "I will see you two later today."

"Bye Mommy," Lexie said.

Terri left and Cadin asked, "May I help you clean the kitchen before I go?"

"Heaven's no. You have done so much for us, I can't ever begin to repay your kindness," Miss Betty said.

"Thanks for a great breakfast. I'll be calling you soon to check on things," she said. "Will you walk me out, Lexie?"

"Yes, ma'am," she answered and pushed away from the table.

They walked out to the bike and Cadin turned to face her and knelt down. "I want you to know how proud of you I am. You're smart, kind, and a hard worker. Don't ever lose those qualities."

"I won't," Lexie said as she started to sniffle. "I love you," she said and rushed into Cadin's arms.

"I love you too," Cadin said as she held the crying child close.

When her tears finally abated, Cadin held her at arm's length. "Be strong and help your mom and Miss Betty as much as you can.

"I will," Lexie said with a smile.

"I'll call you later this week, okay?"

Her smile brightened. "I'd like that."

"Go now and help Miss Betty."

Lexie turned to walk to the house and then rushed back to hug Cadin and kiss her cheek one more time. When she started toward the house, Cadin climbed on the bike and started the motor. She backed the bike to face the drive and waved at Lexie, who had stopped at the door to watch her. With her heart in her throat, Cadin kicked the bike in gear and pulled out of the driveway.

# Chapter Six

The brisk morning wind blew the tears from her eyes as Cadin drove south, away from Greensboro and her new family. The country road she was on was clear of traffic, so she opened the bike's throttle, racing to her next adventure.

When she crested a hill and found a combine moving slowly, she backed off the throttle and maneuvered the bike past the farmer, tossing a wave and a smile his way. His weathered face broke into a smile, and he lifted his sun-darkened hand to return her wave. The fall harvest was well underway and Cadin passed fields freshly plowed, the smell of the turned earth making her think of Miss Betty's garden. With a little attention, it would once more produce a plethora of vegetables to keep her pantry stocked with canned goods.

Cadin never dreamed that such a simple way of life would appeal to her, but her experiences in Greensboro had taught her how therapeutic the slower pace of the country could be for a shattered heart. She opened up the throttle once more and rode another hour before she needed to stop for fuel.

Miss Betty had filled her stomach with a wonderful breakfast before she let her go, but the smells coming from the small country store made Cadin's stomach growl. She filled her tank then went inside to pay for her fuel and investigate what the delicious smells were. A lady working in the small kitchen had just brought out a fresh pan of steaming biscuits as she walked over to the counter. "So that's what smells so good." So many choices made it hard to decide. There was a wide variety of breakfast meats to fill the biscuits and she selected the country ham and smoked sausage.

"May I get you anything else?" the woman asked.

"A bottle of Sun Drop." Cadin grinned. "I haven't had one of those in years."

The woman pulled a chilled bottle of the citrus-flavored drink from a cooler and added it to Cadin's purchases.

Cadin paid the woman and carried her bag of food outside. She pulled her bike over to a small covered picnic table and devoured the two biscuits. A large red-tailed hawk flew into the top of a nearby tree and she crept quietly to her saddlebag to retrieve her camera. The hawk scanned the area for prey as Cadin snapped several shots of the majestic bird. He watched her curiously until a passing truck backfired and he once more took flight to soar across the freshly turned fields.

She reviewed the new pictures she had taken, scrolling through the shots from Terri's birthday party. Cadin's heart soared when she turned to a photo of her and

Lexie sitting on the bike, deep in conversation. Terri must have taken the shot surreptitiously. Lexie was looking up at her with complete adoration as she listened intently to what Cadin was saying. *This one I'll definitely enlarge and frame for home, and my office,* she thought as she scrolled through the rest of the photos.

Draining the last of the Sun Drop, she walked back inside to use the restroom before starting on her way. Passing through the store, she caught the cook's eyes. "Those biscuits were heavenly."

The woman's face lit up with pride. "I'm glad you enjoyed them. Do you want some to go?"

"I'd love some, but my storage space is limited. I will definitely be back for more."

The woman smiled at her. "I'm here every day and we always have fresh biscuits."

"Thanks again," she said and left the store.

She looked up at the cloudless blue sky to see the hawk spiraling down to earth in search of prey. She watched as he dropped to the ground and lifted again, with a small rodent clasped in his talons. "I'm not the only one enjoying a quick snack," she spoke aloud as she settled her helmet on her head and straddled the bike.

†

It was just after two when she arrived in Bogalusa and pulled into a small diner for a late lunch. The crowd was sparse, most of the lunchtime crowd already having rushed back to work or home. She took a seat at a small table and picked up the menu. A small strip of white paper was attached to the menu announcing country fried steak as the daily special, and her mouth instantly watered.

"Welcome. What can I get you to drink?" Cadin heard a slight Creole accent in the server's voice. She looked up into crystal-blue eyes of the woman who had arrived to take her order. "I'll have sweet tea, please. Is the daily special still available?"

"Yes, it is. Are mashed potatoes with gravy and corn good for you?" the woman asked.

"That sounds perfect," Cadin said, returning the woman's smile. She watched her as she walked behind the counter and poured a fresh glass of tea to bring to her. The woman's eyes weren't the only beautiful thing about her. Her dark cinnamon skin glowed and a perfect white smile met Cadin's eyes. To say the woman was lovely was a gross understatement. She was beautiful.

The woman placed her tea on the table. "I'll have your food up in just a few minutes. My name is Emma, if you need anything else."

"Thanks," Cadin managed to speak and watched her return to the kitchen. "Down girl," she whispered softly and busied herself checking the messages on her phone.

†

The door chime sounded as Emma placed a steaming plate of food in front of her. "Here you go. Is there anything else I can get for you now?"

"Not yet," Cadin said. "Those pies look interesting, though," she said, pointing her fork at the display on the counter.

"Just let me know when you're ready."

"I will," she said and turned to greet her next customer.

"Hi, Hank, I hope you go easy on me today," she spoke to the man standing just inside the door, a metal clipboard in hand. Obviously, he was the local health inspector.

"Hi Emma, I'll be as easy as I can, but you know eventually you're going to have to put some money in this place," he answered.

"When I find that money tree I will gladly upgrade." There was concern in her voice.

"I know you're always clean, but the floor, equipment, and furnishings have been here for ages and there's only so much cleaning can do," he said with compassion.

Cadin continued eating her meal as her gaze moved around the small diner. The place could use some modernization she agreed. She watched Emma and Hank disappear into the kitchen then return several minutes later. Hank made several notes and then tore the top copy off the report he had finished and handed it to her.

"Buy yourself a lottery ticket and maybe you'll get lucky," he said with a smile and left the diner.

Emma looked at Cadin who was watching the interaction closely.

She could see the tears pooling in Emma's eyes, until she turned away and rushed into the kitchen.

When she returned several minutes later, Emma had regained her composure and carried a tray of pie slices to her table with a pitcher of tea. She set the tray on the table for her review while she refilled her tea glass. "What can I tempt you with?" she asked.

*That's an awfully loaded question,* Cadin thought with a smirk. "They all look so good. What do you recommend?"

"My favorite is the coconut cream," Emma said.

"May I ask a favor then?"

"Sure, what is it?"

"Grab two slices and a drink for yourself and join me for a few minutes."

Emma looked around the empty diner and then returned Cadin's smile. "I guess I can do that," she answered.

Cadin watched as she returned to the counter, served two slices of pie, and poured a cup of coffee.

"That was a great meal," she said when Emma returned.

"I'm glad you liked it," Emma said with a smile. "I hope you enjoy the pie too. A local woman bakes them fresh for me every day."

"It looks heavenly," she said, pushing her now empty plate to the side and reaching for the pie. She took a bite and groaned with pleasure. "Beyond heavenly," she crooned.

"I will let Merry know you approve," she said with a grin. "What brings you to Bogalusa?"

"Just visiting for a few days," Cadin answered. "I take it this is your place?"

Emma's face beamed with pride. "Yes, I've had it for about four years now. My husband was killed in action overseas, and his benefits aren't enough for my daughter and me to live a decent life on," she said. "I'm sorry, I shouldn't be boring you with this."

"I'm sorry for your loss. Your story isn't boring either, so don't worry about that. I take it that was your local health inspector?" she said to change the subject.

"Hank, yes, he's a real sweetheart, but if the state inspector shows up we'll both be in big trouble. He's given me about as much rope as he can spare."

Cadin was about to speak when the door chime sounded again. A younger version of Emma walked in carrying an armload of books. Cadin looked at Emma. "She has to be yours."

"Hey baby," she said to the teenager. "Cadin, this is my daughter Meagan. What are you doing here so early?"

"Nice to meet you," the young woman said. "Coach is sick so we didn't have practice today."

"What sport do you play?" Cadin asked.

"Volleyball for our high school team," she said.

"Meagan helps me before and after school, and on weekends," Emma said. "She's a great kid, wants to be a teacher one day."

"Oh yeah, what would you like to teach?"

"High school math and science," Meagan answered. "I graduate this year and hope to be able to take a class or two at the community college until I can afford to go to LSU one day."

A pained look crossed Emma's face. "Maybe I should buy two lottery tickets today," she said.

"What's with the lottery tickets?" Meagan asked, confused.

"Hank came by today," she answered. "I don't know how much longer we can go without making some upgrades."

"Why don't you go ahead and use the money you have saved up to help with my college? I love you, Mom, but five thousand won't get me far, but it may keep the diner open longer."

"There's no way I'm using that money," Emma said. "I'll figure something out."

The smile grew on Cadin's face. "If money wasn't an issue, what would you do here?" she asked.

Emma looked dreamy for a few minutes and Cadin waited for her to answer.

"Get a new coffeepot for starters," Meagan said. "I get burned on that one at least once a week."

"To do it right, we'd probably have to close the place down, gut the interior, and start fresh with new flooring, counters, furnishings, and equipment."

"Any idea how much that cost would entail?"

"Probably fifty thousand at a minimum," Emma said with a sigh.

"Who is a good contractor in the area?"

"Johnny Dubose, I went to school with him."

"Would he treat you fairly?"

"Yes, he would. He's been offering to help me for a year or so, I just don't have the money."

Cadin grew thoughtful for a moment. "What time do you close up tonight?"

"We stop serving at seven and usually get out of here around eight."

"Do you think you could give Johnny a call and see if he would agree to meet with us at eight?"

Emma cocked her head at Cadin's request. "I could, but there's no use in it, I can't come up with that kind of money."

"Yes, you can, but you will have to trust me, a total stranger. You have nothing to lose, but much to gain by setting up this meeting."

"What do you mean?" Emma asked.

"Something better than buying a lottery ticket," she answered cryptically.

She smiled and pulled out a twenty-dollar bill to cover her meal and the pie slices, intentionally not answering the question. The ideas were still forming in her head and she wasn't ready to share her plan. She also handed Emma her business card. "I need to find a hotel, but call me to confirm you have the meeting arranged."

"Two miles down the road there's a fairly new chain hotel. You can probably find a room there."

"Thanks, I'll check it out," she said, and turned to Meagan. "May I give you an assignment too?"

"Sure," Meagan said.

"When you have some down time, make a list of the items you and your mother would like to replace. That will give us some information for our meeting with Johnny."

"That sounds easy enough."

"One last thing," Cadin said. "What's the special tonight?"

Emma chuckled. "Fried pork chops, greens, fried okra, and corn bread."

"Great, I'll see you around six." Cadin started to turn away, but stopped. "Would you have some equipment catalogs you could loan me?"

Emma looked at her for a moment with a look of suspicion. *What do I have to lose but a few worn-out catalogs,* she thought to herself as she eyed the woman and then smiled. "Several," Emma said. "Hang on, and I'll get a few."

Meagan waited until her mom had left the room. "Can you really do this? And why would you? You don't know us, it doesn't make sense."

"Not everything in life makes sense." Cadin smiled. "To answer your question, yes, I can, and I'll tell you how later, but right now I need a room and a shower."

"Awesome," Meagan said. She flipped open a notebook and started making notes.

Emma returned moments later carrying a small stack of catalogs and handed them to Cadin. "Here you go."

"Thanks, I'll see you two later," she said before leaving the diner.

They watched the stranger walk to a motorcycle and then exchanged a look and a shrug of their shoulders. Emma looked at her business card. "A lawyer from Atlanta, what in God's name is she doing here?"

"I guess we'll find out in a couple of hours," Meagan said with an excited grin.

"I guess so," her mom answered and walked toward the kitchen, leaving Meagan frantically scribbling notes.

† 

Cadin rode to the hotel and checked in. She noticed a business center next to the front desk and asked the clerk, "Can guests use the Internet here?"

"Yes, ma'am, the business center is open until eleven each night."

"Great, thanks," she said and carried her bag to her room, tossing it on the bed.

She had a few hours to relax until it was time to return to the diner. She grabbed the stack of catalogs Emma had given her and settled into a recliner to peruse the selection of equipment.

As she flipped through the pages, she jotted down notes on the hotel notepad. The dollar total quickly added up to nearly forty thousand. *Was the diner worth sinking fifty thousand or more into*? She didn't have to think long to determine the answer. *Yes, it most certainly was.* She smiled to herself. One other item she wanted to check, but she would need the Internet to do some research, so she grabbed the pile of catalogs, the notepad and walked to the elevator. Emma called just as she stepped off the elevator. "Johnny will be here at eight," she said, the excitement evident in her voice.

"Great, I'll see you soon," Cadin said.

She used her room key to open the business center and sat at a computer. After a few short keystrokes, she pulled up the website for LSU. College tuition sure had increased since she had graduated. She calculated a four-year, prepaid tuition would cost ninety thousand dollars if paid in full. Otherwise, it would cost over one hundred twenty thousand dollars. She printed out the invoice and contact information, folding it in quarters and slipping it into her back pocket. The physician's personal payment would be due in a few short months, on the anniversary of Missy's death. It wasn't hard for her to determine the use of the money. His actions had ruined one life and it was fitting that he would pay to establish another young woman's future.

Back in her room, she pulled out fresh clothing and took a quick shower, her excitement growing by the minute. Cadin dressed and walked to the foyer where a large roadmap hung on the wall. Baton Rouge was only a few hours away. "Time for road trip," she said, and whistled a happy tune as she walked out to her bike.

†

She parked her bike and walked into the crowded diner. It wasn't a four-star restaurant, but the small diner certainly brought in the crowd. Emma smiled when she looked up to see Cadin waiting for a seat behind two couples. Meagan was busing a table while Emma took orders from a family. She spotted an empty seat at the counter and asked the couples ahead of her, "Would you mind if I take that seat at the counter?"

"Heaven's no," one of the men said. "As long as you don't order the last of the pork chops," he added.

Emma heard his exchange. "We have plenty, Harvey," she said.

Cadin walked past them and sat beside a young man who was thoroughly enjoying his meal.

"Hi," he said when she sat next to him.

"Hey, that looks delicious."

"It's so good I'm thinking of ordering seconds," he said.

"Whoa, where's Emma, I need to get an order in ahead of you," she teased.

The man grinned at her and wiped his hands before offering one to Cadin. "Johnny Dubose."

"Cadin Michaels," she answered as she shook his calloused hand. "I believe we have a meeting later."

"Pleased to meet you," he said. "Emma didn't give me many details, but she sure sounded excited."

"I hope after tonight things will be clear for all of us," Cadin said. "Are you very busy right now?"

He smiled. "My crew just finished a major job, and we have two weeks before our next project starts. Some of the boys are going fishing for a few days."

"How many men would you need to gut the flooring and equipment here?"

"I'd have more than enough. It would take a few days though, so Emma would have to close."

"Would the town starve if she closed for a few days?" Cadin said as she looked at the crowd.

"No, but you wouldn't know listening to her customers. Most of these folks eat here several nights a week," Johnny said. "I guess they'd have to fend for themselves. Me included," he added with a grin.

Cadin nodded to the stack of catalogs. "I've got a fair estimate on the equipment costs, but I need to know the construction costs, if you're interested in a project."

"You bet I am," he said. "Emma's a good woman and a hard worker who deserves a break."

"I have every intention of providing that for her," Cadin said.

Johnny gave her a warm smile. "I find it refreshing that a total stranger would even offer her the chance to save her business. What's in it for you?"

"That my new friend, you will have to wait until closing to find out," she said as Emma arrived to take her order.

"I see you've met Johnny."

"Yes, I have. We're already talking about you," Cadin said.

"Ha, juicy stuff I hope," she said. "Do I even need to ask what you want to eat?"

"No, ma'am, that special sounds and looks perfect for me."

"Okay, one special, with a glass of sweet tea, coming right up. Are you up for seconds, Johnny?"

"You must be reading my mind," he said.

They watched as she walked into the kitchen, then Johnny turned back to Cadin. "What kind of flooring did you have in mind?"

"Whatever you think is best, something relatively maintenance free and durable."

"I've got some commercial grade samples out in my truck that I'll bring in when things slow down a bit."

"What do you think about this counter? Pre-fab or custom built?"

"I can build her a beautiful counter and it will last much longer than any pre-fab counter you can buy. I've got a carpenter that will love the task."

"I've noticed most of these companies are in New Orleans. Is there anyone local?"

"Not that can get the items we need quickly. I've got trailers and men who would love a trip to New Orleans to pick up the pieces we need. That's going to be our best bet. To expedite shipping would cost and arm and a leg, and would be an unnecessary cost."

"What about bathrooms?" she asked.

"Have you seen them?" he asked with a grimace.

"No, let's go look while we're waiting on food," she said.

They opened the ladies' room door first and peeked inside. "I see what you mean."

"The men's is even worse. I think the urinal would qualify as an antique," he said with a grin.

"Um, I'll take your word on that." She grinned back at him. "Add the bathrooms in for a full remodel."

"Cha-ching," Johnny said with a boyish grin. "What kind of construction budget are we looking at?"

"I don't know yet. That will be up to you to come up with."

"I'll start working on some figures when we finish eating," he said as they walked back into the dining room as Meagan delivered their plates.

"Enjoy," she said and went to bus more tables as couples continued to come through the door for the next half hour.

✝

Cadin finished her meal and surveyed the room while Emma and Meagan raced to serve the guests. She followed Emma to the kitchen and asked, "Do you mind if I look around a bit?"

"Not at all, make yourself at home. This is Toni, she's our evening cook," Emma said.

"Thanks for a great meal then," Cadin said. "I'll stay out of your way. I just want to look around."

The dishwashing machine and deep fryer looked fairly new compared to the other equipment and the small walk-in cooler was new. The tile flooring was in good shape with the exception of a few areas that needed new grouting. "Not too bad," Cadin said to herself.

Johnny had a notepad and was furiously writing notes so Cadin sat and allowed her eyes to survey the room. Her eyes landed on the booths lining the back wall. The upholstery appeared heavily worn and Cadin surmised they would cost more to re-cover them than they were worth. She was curious if Emma would want to purchase more booths or go strictly with tables. It would increase the seating capacity in addition to making the diner more modern looking.

✝

When the last customers had left, Emma locked the front door and turned over the Closed sign. Meagan and Toni busied themselves with the cleanup as Emma joined Johnny and Cadin.

"What a night," she said, taking a deep breath. "Do y'all want to move to a table so you can spread out?"

"That's probably not a bad idea," Johnny said.

"Did you and Meagan have a chance to work on a list of equipment?" Cadin asked.

"Yes, we did," Emma said and pulled a folded paper from her apron.

"Let's start with the furniture here. What would you like to do?" Cadin asked.

"Use these old booths for a bonfire for starters," Emma said, much to Cadin's relief.

"That's what I was thinking too. If you went with tables only, you can drastically increase your seating capacity."

"Those old monsters are almost impossible to clean under too," Meagan chimed in from behind the counter.

Cadin pushed the stack of catalogs over to Emma. "Let's start with tables and chairs then. Pick out what you'd like. Johnny, may I have a few pieces of paper?"

"Sure thing." He tore off several sheets from his notepad and handed them to her as Emma started looking through the catalogs.

"Nothing red please, Mom, I'm sick of red," Meagan said.

"What color then, sweetheart?"

"Something blue would be nice."

"Take a break and come look at these," Emma said.

Meagan dropped the cleaning cloth she was using to wipe down the tables, and came over to stand behind her mother. "I like those," she said, pointing out the exact tables

Emma had been returning to as she flipped through the pages.

"That was easy enough, now how many tables and chairs?" Cadin said as she wrote down the page and item numbers of the tables and then the chairs they selected to match. "Is there a soup kitchen or a homeless shelter that could use these tables and chairs?"

"Yes, to both and they would probably love to have them, but you're talking about replacing all of them?"

"Yes, all new to match. You probably need to order a dozen extra chairs for spares."

"Cool," Meagan said and returned to cleaning.

"Finish wiping things down and I'll mop in the morning," Emma told her daughter.

"I'll come in early and help you, Mom," Meagan said.

"Thanks baby," Emma said and turned to see Cadin watching them with a smile.

"Johnny, can you bring in those flooring samples for us to look over?" Cadin asked.

"Yes, thanks for reminding me," he said.

"Let's take a look at your equipment list, while he's outside," she said.

A new coffeemaker in large letters topped the list. "I see what Meagan's first choice is," Cadin teased. "Has she picked one out?"

"She certainly has," Emma chuckled and pointed it out for Cadin, who added it to her list.

Johnny returned and placed a bundle of floor tile samples on the table. "Any of these will work well for both here and the bathrooms," he said. "I've already included some water saving toilets, a urinal, and new sinks on my list.

I'll do some rough measurements while you ladies pick out the tile."

"Wow, so many choices," Emma stated, a bit overwhelmed.

"Well, I think it's safe to rule out any reds," Cadin said.

"Yes, I'd have to agree with that. Something with some blue in it to pull out the table coloring would work."

By the time Meagan finished her cleaning they had it narrowed down to three choices. "Which of these do you like?" Emma asked.

Meagan chuckled. "Any of them would be better than what we have."

"I know that, but which would you prefer?"

She surprised them by selecting an off-white base with blue, green, and gray flecks. "This would pull out the blue of the tables and still add additional color," she said.

"That's a great choice and it looks beautiful when it's down," Johnny said, returning from measuring the bathrooms. "I have leftovers from a previous job that I would love to get out of my storage, so we don't have to buy as much."

"That's decided then," Emma said.

Johnny continued figuring the construction costs while Emma, Meagan, and Cadin selected the rest of the equipment. Toni finished in the kitchen and called out goodnight as she left out the back door.

Cadin busied herself adding up the equipment costs as Johnny finished the quote for construction. "What will it cost to close down for three days?" Cadin asked.

"Oh my, I hadn't thought about that," Emma said. She estimated the daily take and Cadin multiplied by three and added it into the costs.

Cadin was surprised the equipment costs came in lower than she expected, and she waited for Johnny to finish his totals. Emma and Meagan looked on nervously.

Johnny finally turned his quote sheet over to show Cadin and she combined the two figures, for a total of sixty-three thousand dollars.

"That includes an extra five thousand in case we run into problems with plumbing or have to change materials for some reason so it could be lower," he said.

"That's a lot of money," Emma said, disappointment evident in her voice.

Cadin pushed back slightly from the table and looked at Emma. "Now is the time for us to talk business." She took a deep breath and released it slowly. "I would like to offer to finance the remodeling for you. I have a few requirements that must be met, but first I have to tell you a story."

Emma, Meagan, and Johnny sat patiently while she told them about Missy's death and the foundation. Both Meagan and Emma had tears in their eyes when she finished, and Johnny found it difficult to hide his emotions as well.

"The most important requirement for me is the name of the diner. Would you object to calling it Missy's Place?" Cadin asked.

"Not at all, I think given the circumstances and your generous offer, that's the least we could do for you," Emma said.

Meagan surprised her with a request. "Could we get a picture of Missy to hang up by the register?"

Cadin felt her heart choking off her throat. Meagan had asked for something she hadn't given any consideration to, and she loved the idea. She nodded her head in agreement. "That's a great idea," she said when she could finally speak. "There is one final piece we need to discuss,"

Cadin said. "You will need to hire someone to replace Meagan next fall."

Meagan looked at her mother completely puzzled. Emma shrugged her shoulders. "Why is that necessary?" she finally asked Cadin.

"Because," Cadin said as she pulled the paper from her back pocket, "you will be moving out."

Meagan just chuckled. "Yeah right, where am I going?" she joked.

Cadin unfolded the paper she placed in front of Meagan. "You'll be going to Baton Rouge to attend LSU."

"What?" Meagan screamed and jumped out of her seat, knocking over the chair she had been sitting on.

"The foundation will be purchasing a prepaid college plan for you as soon as I can ride to Baton Rouge. I will also match what you can save this year for living expenses."

"No way, you have to be joking," Meagan said.

Cadin shook her head. "No, I'm not. Missy would love the fact that she could help you become a schoolteacher," Cadin said.

Both Meagan and her mother broke into tears, leaving Johnny and Cadin speechless.

Cadin busied herself by looking over the numbers they had developed while Meagan and Emma regained control. When they had both wiped away their tears and sat looking at her, Cadin turned to Johnny. "How much do you need to get started?"

"Fifteen will buy the supplies and take care of the demolition."

She pulled out her checkbook and wrote the check, tore it off, and handed it to him. She then looked at Emma. "When do you want to get started?"

She stared at Cadin for a few seconds as reality sank into her brain. "This is really happening."

"Yes, it is," she answered. "I assume you will need to post a sign on the door that the diner will be closing for a few days."

Emma nodded. "Yes. I'll do that tomorrow. Can we order the equipment tomorrow?"

Johnny spoke up. "I told Cadin that I'd have some of my boys go down to New Orleans to pick up the order to expedite it without the huge shipping costs."

"Thank you Johnny, and thank you Cadin."

Johnny nodded as Cadin said, "You're welcome." She looked at Johnny then back to Emma. "Is there anything else we need to cover tonight?"

"Not from my end. I'll call my crew and get them set up to start the demolition Friday, if that's good for you Emma."

Still in a bit of shock, Emma looked up at him. "Yes, Friday will be fine. I'll post the notice in the morning."

"I'll pull the permits and order the supplies we need tomorrow. Just let me know when and where to send the crew for the equipment."

"What's a good time to come in to place the order with you?" she asked Emma.

"The breakfast rush is usually over by nine."

"I'll see you at eight then for breakfast," Cadin said, standing. "I think we've got a good plan." Saying good night she walked out the front door. Out on the sidewalk, she looked through the front window to see the three of them watching her, mouths slightly agape as she walked by. She lifted her hand to wave goodbye and felt her smile growing as she reached her bike.

Cadin rode the short distance to the hotel and entered her room. She undressed and prepared for bed. Sliding onto the cool sheets, Cadin fell asleep feeling totally at peace for the first time in a long time.

# Chapter Seven

Cadin took a long, relaxing shower before dressing and riding to the diner for a late breakfast. As she rode through the small town, she noted the location of a major bank and a branch of her cellular carrier. She pulled into the latter and went inside to purchase a simple to use cell phone, adding it to her account. She would send it to Terri for Lexie to keep in touch with her in the next day or so.

†

She smiled as she reached the front door and read the sign announcing the closure for remodeling. There was a couple eating breakfast when Cadin walked inside. Emma looked up to see her enter and her face beamed with excitement.

"Good morning."

"A great morning indeed, I hope you slept well," Emma said.

"Like a rock."

"What can I get you for breakfast?" Emma said as she poured a fresh cup of coffee and placed it in front of Cadin.

Cadin thought for a second then said, "Two eggs, over easy, bacon, hash browns, and rye toast, a glass of apple juice if you have it too, please."

"Coming right up then," Emma said and relayed the order to Toni who had volunteered to come in and help while Emma planned for the remodel.

"How has your morning been?"

"Busy, and filled with a million questions about why the diner will be closed. Everyone is excited about the remodeling."

"That's good. People will be eager to see how the new place looks when we're done."

"I want you to know, Meagan barely slept last night. She is so excited to be going off to LSU. I can't thank you enough for that."

"Such eagerness to teach should not go untapped," Cadin said.

The couple finished their meal and walked to the cash register to pay. Emma thanked them for their business and then walked back to the window to retrieve Cadin's breakfast. She placed the platter of food in front of Cadin. "Would you mind if I start calling in the order while you eat?"

"Heaven's no, go ahead. Be sure and get a total and ask if they need a certified check," Cadin said as she seasoned her breakfast.

Emma pulled a phone from under the counter and placed it next to Cadin then got the list they had developed the previous night. She placed the paper on the counter and looked at Cadin.

"Go ahead," Cadin encouraged her, then took a bite of the food.

Emma let out a deep breath, opened a line on the speakerphone and dialed the number. Minutes later, she was busy making their order and speaking to the representative about arrangements for taking delivery of the equipment.

"Would you mind if I put you on hold to make sure we have everything in stock and total the order for you?" the woman asked.

"No problem," Emma said and took the opportunity to retrieve a pot of coffee to freshen up their cups.

"Thanks," Cadin whispered.

"You're welcome," Emma whispered back with a giggle.

"Thank you for holding, Ms. Lewis," the woman said when she returned to the line. "We have everything in stock for you and several of the items are on sale. If you're ready to finalize the order, we will have everything ready for pickup Friday morning."

Emma looked at Cadin who nodded to her. "Go ahead and place the order," she said.

The woman finished getting contact information and then gave Emma a revised total, which was almost five thousand less than what they had calculated. When Emma ended the call, she looked up to a smiling Cadin.

"That was much better than we anticipated."

"Yes, it was, so how about some fresh paint and some new dishes?" Cadin said.

"Dishes we can get locally and I'm sure Johnny can recommend a painter."

"I'll leave those two tasks for you to arrange then," Cadin said. "Make me a copy of the total, the name of the company and I'll get a check from the bank."

Emma took out her order pad and wrote down the information Cadin needed.

"I will also need personal information for Meagan. I plan on riding to Baton Rouge tomorrow to get her plan finalized."

"What will you need?"

"Her full name, date of birth, social security number, addresses, and contact information. If I need anything else, I'll give you a call."

Emma jotted down the information as requested.

"Has Meagan applied to LSU for admission?"

"No, until last night she didn't think it was possible."

Cadin remained silent for a few minutes. "Is there a rental car company in town?"

"Yes, you can access them from your hotel," Emma said.

"Would you mind if Meagan played hooky from school tomorrow and went to Baton Rouge with me?"

"That's fine with me as long as she doesn't have any tests tomorrow. She should be here around four after practice tonight."

"I guess I should ask if you'd mind if I help her get her application arranged. We can wait until the work starts if you want to go with us."

"I would like that," Emma said. "Could we go Friday when they start the demolition?"

"I like that idea better. I'll make the arrangements with the university," Cadin said.

"Thank you. I know that day will be a big step for Meagan and I really should be there."

"You are absolutely right."

"So what are you going to do the rest of today?"

"I'm going to go to the bank to take care of the check, and I thought I'd go for a ride to see some of the countryside."

"Will you stop in for lunch?"

Cadin grinned. "Just try keeping me away from here during mealtime."

"Well, I guess we need to make some alternative plans for the weekend then. How about having dinner at our place Saturday night?"

"How can I say no to that?" Cadin finished her glass of juice.

"Is there anything else I can get you?"

"Just the check," Cadin said as she pulled out some cash.

"You've got to be kidding me. You won't pay for another meal here again," Emma said, placing her hands on her hips.

"Thanks. I guess I'll see you for lunch."

Cadin walked out to her bike and rode to the bank. Twenty minutes later she emerged from the bank with the certified check and climbed back on her bike to head out of town. Traffic was light as she drove west toward bayou country. The moss-draped oaks gave way to cypress, buried to their knobby knees in the murky water as she rode through the bayous. She made several stops to take pictures of the majestic views, and when she stopped on a bridge, Cadin sat quietly on the concrete wall to watch and listen to the creatures of the swamp. A crane waded through the water with his awkward stride. Cadin watched as he submerged his head, lifting it seconds later, beak filled with a small fish, frog, or crawfish that quickly disappeared down his throat. Her camera captured several frames of his hunt, her grin growing behind the lens until a loud splash caught her attention. She swung the camera around to the direction of the sound and gasped when the lens found a large alligator swimming in the direction of the crane.

The crane, sensing he was in imminent danger, took flight when the alligator was ten feet away and flew to a branch out of the reptile's reach. "That was close," she spoke aloud as she watched the alligator turn and lazily make his way back to sun himself on the bank.

Cadin rode several miles down the highway until she saw a rusted sign advertising an alligator farm and airboat rides. She slowed when she reached the turnoff and grinned to herself. "That's too good of a combination to turn down." She followed the signs deeper into the bayou and breathed a sigh of relief when several small buildings came into view. She pulled her bike to a halt and cut the engine.

"I thought I heard a motorbike," a voice called from the side of one of the buildings.

Cadin watched as a small-framed man appeared and offered her a broad smile. "I can't say when I've seen such a pretty lady riding a motorbike," he said, obviously flirting.

"Your farm and airboat ride were too tempting to resist," she told him.

"Come with me then, young lady," he said. "My name's Rupert Finley, friends just call me Rupe."

"I'm Cadin," she told him as she followed him around the building. "What do you do with the gators you raise?"

Rupe grinned at her. "Most of them I sell to Fish and Wildlife to replenish lakes and bayous that get fished out. Others I sell to local meat vendors for the meat and hides."

"I don't think I've ever eaten alligator," she remarked.

"You should try some while you're visiting the area, it can be quite tasty, and no, before you ask, it doesn't taste like chicken," he said with a chuckle.

"How did you know I was going to ask?" Cadin teased him.

"It's one of the most common questions I get asked by visitors." He grinned, revealing several missing teeth.

They walked down a wooden trail. "These pens hold some of the older critters that I keep for breeding."

Cadin peered into the "pens," which were nothing more than wire barriers separating sections of the swamp. Each pen held gators of similar size, and growing in length the further they walked down the path. "How do you keep them fed? I bet they can consume a great deal of food."

"The design allows fish and other small creatures to enter the pens. Also, I get outdated meats from local grocery stores and the county brings out the roadkill they scoop up from the roads."

She grimaced at the mention of roadkill. "That has to be a shitty job," she said.

"Not glamorous by any means, but necessary. Thankfully it's handled on a regular basis. You sure don't want to roll up on a gator feasting on a dead coon in the middle of the highway, especially on that motorbike of yours."

"You have a very good point there," she agreed. "I hadn't thought of it in that light."

"I also have several young boys who like to hunt for nutria," he said. "They're not much for eating, but they are plentiful in the swamps."

"What is nutria?"

"We call them swamp rats. They were brought into the area hundreds of years ago, bred for their pelts, but today they're only seen as a nuisance. Many of them escaped captivity and unchecked, they soon overpopulated the area." He chuckled. "They breed like rabbits, and love to raid crawfish traps, so fishermen pay local kids to hunt them down to prevent depleting the crawfish in the area."

"So the fishermen pay the kids for killing them, and then the kids bring them to you, and you pay them for the meat?"

"You got it, missy. The gators get fed, the crawfish are safe, and the teenagers have some jingle in their pockets."

"That's very smart."

"That's the way of the bayou."

At the end of the path were numerous fiberglass containers. Croaking sounds could be heard from twenty feet away, as they approached.

"Those are the babies," he said when she looked at him. "Once they are hatched, I have to get them away from the male gators or else they will end up as a snack. So I round up as many as I can, and they live here until they are big enough to be released into a larger pen."

Cadin looked over the edge of the nearest containers. Each one held babies of different sizes from six inches long to several feet. "They look harmless at this size."

"Don't be fooled, those teeth can already do major damage," he warned.

She looked up from the containers to follow his movement as he walked to an airboat.

"I was just about to go out and check some traps for lunch, if you want to ride. Isn't exactly a tour, but you'll see plenty of gators."

"I'd love it," Cadin said. "What are you trapping for lunch?"

"Hopefully some crawfish. If I don't have any in the traps, I can always check my float lines for some catfish. I always keep a fish or two on the lines."

"The swamp provides a lot for you doesn't it?"

"It's been my way of life since I was a young man. It provides my income and generally feeds me. I keep some burger patties in the freezer, in case of emergencies."

Cadin followed him onto the boat and sat in a bucket seat. "Better strap in and put these on," he said, handing her a protective headset for her ears. He cranked the powerful motor.

Even with protection, she could hear the roar of the motor as he gave the boat gas and they sped away from the dock. She let out a gasp of surprise at the speed in which they departed the farm and settled into her seat.

Rupe expertly propelled the boat through the swamp. She looked to her right as he slowed when he reached an area that was home to several large alligators. "There are some big boys sunning on the bank," he said, pointing them out to her.

She saw their hides coated in mud, camouflaging them in the weedy banks. They remained so still Cadin had to strain her eyes to see them. They were huge, well over ten feet long. "Holy cow," she said and turned to see Rupe smiling.

He nodded and increased speed and then turned down a canal and cut the motor, guiding the boat toward a tree. "Let's see if Rupe's got lunch," he said as he moved to the front of the boat and grabbed a tree branch to slow the approach. His hand found the cable attached to a wire trap, pulled it from the water, and balanced it on the edge of the boat to allow the water to drain from the trap.

Cadin saw the trap half full of tiny lobster-looking creatures.

"Oh yeah, Rupe's gonna have some mudbugs," he said as he opened the top of the trap and dumped the contents into a five-gallon bucket.

"Now those I have had in Atlanta," Cadin told him.

"I guarantee they don't taste as good in Atlanta."

"You're probably right. I will have to try those too, before I head back to Atlanta."

Rupe cocked his head and looked at her. "What brings you to the bayou from Atlanta?"

"I'm just taking some time to see some of the country," she answered.

He shook his head. "I don't see how folks can live in those big cities."

"It's a different world out here, that's for sure," Cadin said. "I've really enjoyed being away from the city."

"Not a bad place to hang your hat and call home."

"No, sir, not at all," she answered.

"You want to see more of the bayou?"

Her face lit up with excitement. "Yes, if you have the time."

Rupe laughed. "I always have time for the bayou."

He started the motor and gave her a proper tour of his bayou. When she saw the farm come into sight, Cadin was disappointed the ride was over. Rupe killed the motor and pulled up to the dock. He secured the boat and offered her his hand. "Careful now, this isn't the spot to go for a swim," he teased.

She took off the headset and placed it on the seat before taking his hand and stepping carefully onto the dock. Rupe picked up the bucket holding his lunch and joined her on the dock. "Would you care to join me for lunch?"

"I would love to, but I already have a commitment in Bogalusa," she said.

"Thanks for coming by then and have a safe ride back," he said as they walked back to the main building.

"What do I owe you for the tour?"

"Wasn't really a tour," he said.

"It was your time and fuel. That's not free. Will this cover it?" she asked, handing him two twenties.

"I can't take that from you, missy."

"Think of it as a down payment for lunch and Abitas next time I come through then," she said.

"You have a deal," he said and pocketed her money. "Do come back when you can."

"I will," Cadin said and strolled to her bike.

Rupe waved and watched her ride away.

† 

Cadin opened up the bike on the return trip, and made it back to Bogalusa at one.

"Welcome back," Emma said as she entered the diner.

"Thanks, I hope you have something good for lunch. I passed up on mudbugs," she said with a grin.

"Well, I don't have mudbugs, but I think I can find something you'll eat around here. Where did you go?"

"I'm not actually sure, but I spent an enjoyable morning with a man named Rupe on his alligator farm and he took me on an airboat ride."

"Those are always fun," Emma said. "What are you hungry for? We had turkey clubs and fries for the special today."

"That will work for me."

"I think I'll join you," Emma said.

The door opened and Johnny walked into the diner. "You have any food left?"

"Of course, come on in. I was about to make turkey clubs and fries for Cadin and me. Does that suit you or do you want something heavier?"

"That'll do just fine," he said and took a seat by Cadin. "How are you today?"

"Doing great thanks, and you?"

"Fantastic, I'm ready to start ripping this place apart."

"Hey now, not for another day yet," Emma hollered from the kitchen.

"I got a lot done this morning. Everything's ordered, got the permits and the crew will be here at six Friday morning to do the demolition."

"Do you have painters on your crew?" Cadin asked.

"Sure do, we going to paint too?"

"Emma got such a good deal on the equipment, that we had money left over from the budget."

Emma returned carrying the first two plates. "What color would you suggest?" she asked him.

"I'd stick to an off-white close to the base of the tile to make the room appear larger and lighter," he said. "You can always add decorations to bring in some color."

She poured three glasses of tea and returned to the kitchen for her plate. Before she took her seat she reached under the counter for a keychain and handed it to him

"What's this?"

"You will need a key to the front door, so you can get inside Friday. Meagan and I are going to Baton Rouge with Cadin to get her registered for college."

"That's great news. By the time y'all make it back, you will see how much we were able to get done."

Cadin reached into her pocket and pulled out her wallet. "Before I forget, here's the check for the equipment. It will be ready Friday morning."

Johnny tucked the check away in his wallet. "Will you call the shelter and see if they can come pick up the tables and chairs after you close Thursday night? I can provide some muscle if they need help loading," he offered.

"I'll give them a call this afternoon," Emma said.

"What about the booths?" Cadin asked.

"I'm having a construction Dumpster delivered Thursday night. We'll toss them in there with the other demolition materials."

†

Meagan walked in as they were finishing their lunch. "You're here early."

"I know, Mom, Coach is still out sick."

"What does your Friday look like?"

"Nothing special, classes as usual."

"No tests or anything you can't miss?"

"No, ma'am, why?" she asked.

"Because you're playing hooky and we're going to Baton Rouge with Cadin. We need to get your application in and get you set for college in the fall."

"Awesome," she said and gave her mom a high five. She turned to Cadin. "I talked with my counselor today and she's going to start an application to LSU for me. I'll let her know we're going up Friday so we can have it ready to go."

"That will make the trip go faster," Cadin said. "We can look at housing options while we're there since they are limited on dorm rooms."

"I can help with that," Johnny piped in. "I have an aunt who lives near campus and would love to rent you a room."

Meagan let out a squeal of excitement and clapped her hands.

"See, honey everything is falling into place," Emma said. "Could we meet with your aunt Friday?"

"I'll get it arranged for you and call you with the address."

"Thanks," Meagan said and hugged his neck.

"Hey, what's the dinner special tonight?" he asked.

"Country fried steak, and mashed potatoes with bacon gravy, fresh green beans, and hot rolls," Emma said.

"I'd better get to peeling potatoes then," Meagan said.

"I'll start snapping the beans in a bit," Emma said.

"I can help with that," Cadin said. "I don't have plans for the rest of the afternoon."

"I think that's my cue to leave," Johnny said. "I'll get the painters arranged and see you around six."

"Later, Johnny," Emma said after ringing up his meal and giving him change.

*Ali Spooner*

†

Cadin spent the afternoon snapping beans and helping
Emma and Meagan in the kitchen, Toni, the main cook, was
due back to work at three, and they had put together a good
start to the dinner special by the time she arrived.

Emma cracked up laughing when she placed the
beans in a pressure cooker and Cadin suddenly decided it
was time to leave the kitchen. "What's wrong?"

"My grandma used one of those when I was growing
up, and I was terrified the thing would explode. That danged
jiggler's noise gives me the creeps."

"Actually they are relatively safe, as long as you pay
proper attention. They will give these beans a great start to
cooking and then I'll finish them off on the stove."

"You go right ahead then. Do you have something I
can do on the other side of the kitchen?"

Emma stifled her laughing to answer. "You can fry
up some bacon that we'll use in the gravy, so don't throw
away the grease."

"I'm all over it, boss," Cadin answered and went to
work. She found that she was enjoying the time spent in the
kitchen with the others, but learned a life in a diner kitchen
wasn't something she wanted to do full time. Still, it was a
great way to see how hard Emma and Meagan worked to
make ends meet.

When they finished all the prep work for dinner,
Emma looked at Cadin. "Thanks for your help, but it's time
for you to take a break."

Cadin wiped the sweat from her brow. "I won't argue
with you at all. That's hard work."

Emma led them to the counter for a glass of tea. "I
reckon I've just gotten used to the work."

144

Cadin was about to comment when the door opened and a young woman entered carrying a dusty backpack. "Are you still open?"

"Yes, come on in, we are about to start serving dinner," Emma said. "You look a bit thirsty."

"Yes, ma'am, I've been walking all day. I'd love some sweet tea if you have it."

Emma chuckled. "I'd have to close down if I didn't." Emma showed her to a table and handed her a menu.

The young woman grinned back at her. "I reckon so," she said as she accepted the menu.

"It's none of my business, but are you traveling alone?"

The woman sat up straighter in her seat. "Yes, I am. I've been on the road for a few weeks now."

Cadin heard the woman's response and turned to give her a closer look. She would be surprised if she were twenty years old. She was lean and dusty from the road, looking like she could use a hot shower and a few good meals.

"Isn't it dangerous being alone?" Emma asked.

"It can be if you aren't careful."

"I'd be scared to death if my daughter was out on her own like that," Emma said.

Cadin watched as the woman's eyes cringed with anger or maybe hurt. "That's a big difference between you and my mama then, she could care less."

"Are you talking about me again, Mama?" Meagan said as she walked out of the kitchen.

The young woman's eyes widened and she smiled at Meagan. "Hey," she said as Meagan approached.

"Hey, yourself," Meagan answered.

"Like I said, we are about to get ready to serve dinner, so you are welcome to join us," Emma said, looking between her daughter and the young woman.

"That would be great," she answered, not taking her eyes off Meagan.

"We have a really good special tonight," Meagan said.

"Anything hot will be a blessing. My name's Serena."

"I'm Meagan and this is my mom, Emma, and our friend Cadin," she said, nodding toward Cadin, who had turned in her seat. "She's a traveler too," Meagan said.

"Is that your bike out front?" she asked as Cadin approached.

"Yes, ma'am, it is," she said as she took a seat at the table.

"Let's get some food out here," Emma said to Meagan.

Serena watched them return to the kitchen and then turned to find Cadin watching her. "So, where are you from?"

"A little town called Moscow in Tennessee," she answered. "I left there about three weeks ago."

"What made you leave home?"

"My mama's new boyfriend; he wanted a group package," she sneered. "I'm not into boys and especially not greasy old men."

Cadin chuckled. "I can appreciate that. So where are you headed?"

Serena shrugged. "I thought I might head down to New Orleans. I hear people are a little more tolerant of my kind there."

"That's not a place to be if you plan on living on the street," Emma said as she carried out two plates with Meagan right behind her with two more.

"I hope I can find some work and a place to stay, but if not I'll just keep moving."

"Emma is right, it's very dangerous to be traveling alone," Cadin said.

"Probably not any less dangerous than staying at home," Serena answered.

"Enough serious talk for now," Emma said. "Let's eat before the dinner crowd arrives."

The food, as usual, was delicious and Cadin watched Serena attack her meal with gusto. "How long has it been since you've had a hot meal?"

"A couple of weeks, I've been living on potted meat and crackers. This food is beyond delicious, reminds me of my grandma's cooking."

Emma smiled at the praise. "What kind of work can you do?"

"I've done waitressing at a truck stop, but I can wash dishes, bus tables, and I'm a decent breakfast cook."

Cadin's eyes caught Emma's with a smile as they both had similar thoughts.

"Could you eat a second plate?" Cadin asked.

Serena hung her head. "Yes, but I can't afford another."

"That's not what I asked," she said.

"Yes, I could eat another, ma'am."

"Don't ma'am me, I'm not that old yet," Cadin said. "Meagan, will you bring another plate?"

"Yes, ma'am," she said, and Cadin shot her a grin.

When Emma finished her meal, she stood to clear some of the plates. Cadin picked up a handful and followed her into the kitchen. She set the plates on the bus cart and turned to look at Emma. "Are you thinking what I'm thinking?"

"That I should hire her to help around here," Emma answered.

Cadin's grin answered her question. "What do you think?"

"Normally I would be wary of hiring a total stranger, but your appearance has taught me that strangers can turn out well. You seem to be a good judge of people. Do you believe her story?"

"No warning whistles are going off in my head. She's seems to be in a tough spot, and I'd hate to see her end up on the streets of New Orleans."

"Do you think I should give her a try?"

"We only have one day left before demolition begins, but I'd vote yes, if I have a vote that is," Cadin answered. "I'll get her a room tonight so she can get cleaned up and do some laundry if needed. Is there someplace she can rent afterward if she works out?"

"I have an extra room. I'll talk it over tonight with Meagan and see what she thinks about Serena staying with us at least temporarily."

"May I make a suggestion then?"

"Sure, you've done right by me so far." She grinned.

"If she works well tomorrow, offer her a place rent free, but she works for tips in lieu of paying rent."

Emma's eyes lit up. "That's a great idea."

"Offer a trial workday tomorrow and I'll take care of her tonight and tomorrow night. If you get a good feeling for her tomorrow and Meagan's okay with her moving in you can make the offer then."

"That sounds like a plan. Will you get her here by six?"

"Is breakfast included?"

"You know it is," Emma said.

Meagan walked into the kitchen at that moment. "You know, Mom, I was thinking," she said.

"Yes, dear," Emma said with a wink to Cadin.

"Well, you know Cadin said you'd need to hire someone to replace me, so why not Serena? She has experience and seems nice."

Cadin was the first to break out in laughter.

Meagan looked at her and then at her smiling mother.

"We were just discussing the same thing," Emma said and Meagan joined in the laughter.

"Great minds think alike," Cadin said. "Now who has room for some apple pie?" she asked.

"Obviously you do," Emma said. "Grab a pie and I'll bring some plates. Meagan, grab the tea pitcher."

Cadin carried the pie to the table. "Are ready for dessert?"

"I'm stuffed," Serena said then saw the pie Cadin placed on the table. "That looks good though."

"Maybe just a little piece then," Cadin said.

Meagan served the pie as Emma turned to Serena. "We have an idea to run past you," she said. "Meagan will be going off to college next fall and I need someone to help me during the day now while she's in school. Would you be interested in working here?"

Serena nearly choked on the bite of pie she was gulping down. "Yes, ma'am, I'd like to give it a try."

"Fine then," Emma said. "Cadin's going to get you a room for two nights at the hotel she's staying in to get cleaned up and a good night's rest. She will bring you back at six in the morning and we'll see how you do."

Tears filled her eyes as Serena looked from one face to the next. "You'd really do that for me?"

"I need help and you need a job," Emma said.

"Thank you," Serena said. "Thank you all."

†

"Have you ridden on a motorcycle before?" Cadin asked as they left the diner.

"Once or twice," she answered.

Cadin straddled the bike and reached for the spare helmet. Her thoughts immediately flew back to the last person to wear it and she thought it was time to call Lexie. She smiled and tossed the helmet to Serena. "Put this on then and hold on tight."

Serena caught the helmet and buckled it before climbing onto the back of the bike. She tentatively placed her hands on Cadin's waist, but gripped her tighter when Cadin started the motor and drove away.

†

"I'm in the room next door if you need anything," Cadin said. "Do you need to do some laundry to have something clean for tomorrow?"

"I have a clean outfit in my bag," Serena answered.

"Have a great night then and I'll see you at five thirty in the lobby."

"Thanks again for everything. I can't wait to get a hot shower."

✝

Cadin sat patiently in the hotel lobby sipping coffee while she waited for Serena to arrive. Five thirty came and went with no sign of the young woman and Cadin began to worry the woman had skipped out on her. Then the elevator bell chimed and Serena came rushing out.

"Sorry, I'm late, I had to dry my hair," she said.

Cadin stared, amazed by the transformation from a road-worn ruffian to the woman standing in front of her. The hot meal, a long shower, and good night's rest had changed Serena's appearance drastically. She had pulled her medium-brown hair back into a ponytail and her eyes sparkled with excitement.

"Let's roll," Cadin said.

✝

When they entered the diner, Meagan and Emma were waiting for them.

"Meagan's going to show you around," Emma said as she poured Cadin a fresh cup of coffee.

"Come on," Meagan said and led Serena into the kitchen.

"She looks completely different all cleaned up," Emma said.

"Your typical girl next door," Cadin said.

"Meagan was excited about Serena staying with us, so I guess today will tell the story."

"I hope she does well. She seems like a good kid."

Their conversation ended when the door chime sounded and the first customers arrived.

✝

Cadin stayed for breakfast and then returned to the hotel after a stop to ship the phone to Terri and Lexie. It was still early morning, but she was sure at least Miss Betty and Terri were awake.

She dialed Miss Betty's number and waited for an answer. Terri picked up on the third ring.

"Good morning."

"Hey, Terri, this is Cadin. I'm calling to check in on everyone."

"Cadin, I'm so glad you called. Lexie has been worried about you. We're all doing fine. How are you?"

"I'm doing great, thanks. Before I forget, expect a package in a couple of days. I'm sending you a cell phone so Lexie can call as often as she likes."

"Within reason though," Terri said with a chuckle. "Talk to Miss Betty for a minute while I go get the sleepyhead out of bed. She'll die if she misses your call."

"Okay, thanks."

"Hello Cadin," Miss Betty said, taking over the phone. "I can't begin to tell you how good it is to be home."

"I'm glad to hear that," Cadin said. She could hear Lexie squealing as she ran into the room, her feet pounding on the floor.

"Here's Lexie, I'll talk to you later. Thanks again, Cadin."

"My pleasure, Miss Betty," she answered.

"Hi Cadin," Lexie's sweet voice said. "I was worried about you."

"I'm sorry, but I got tied up with some things."

"Everything is okay though, right?"

Cadin chuckled softly. "Yes, everything is good. What have you been doing?"

"Brittany and I have been playing every day and she's been introducing me to some of the other kids in town that we'll be going to school with. I'm going to a roller skating party this afternoon too."

"Wow, you've been busy. How are things going at home?"

"It's great being here with Miss Betty. She cooks me breakfast every day. Yesterday she showed me how to make waffles."

"That sounds yummy. You can make me one when I visit."

"Are you coming back soon?"

"I don't know when yet," she answered.

"I hope it's soon. I miss you."

"I miss you and everyone else."

"Please come home soon," Lexie said. "Here's Mommy."

"Hey Cadin, I've got to go to work, but I wanted to thank you again for everything you've done for Lexie and me. Things are really looking great for us here."

"That's excellent news. I'm glad things are going well."

"Will you be headed our way anytime soon?"

"I don't really know yet, but I'll let you know. Please show Lexie how to call me when the phone arrives."

"I will. Bye for now," Terri said and handed the phone back to Lexie.

"Bye Mommy, have a good day," she heard Lexie say before she came back on the phone line.

"Mommy says I need to let you go, but that we'll talk again soon."

"Yes, we will. Have fun at the skating party. Don't fall too much."

Lexie giggled. "I can roller skate, Cadin."

"Cool, I never could do it without bruising my butt," she admitted.

"I'll be careful. I love you, Cadin."

"Love you too, Lexie. Bye for now."

Cadin sat on the end of the bed staring at the phone in her hand for several seconds. She hadn't counted on being sad after talking with Lexie, but the sound of her voice made her heart ache. She decided to get out of the room and take a long ride before going to the diner for lunch and to see how Serena was doing.

†

Cadin turned left when she reached the crossroads heading out of town. As the sun rose higher in the sky the bridges disappeared as the bayous turned into cotton fields. Row after row of white cotton bolls were near fully developed soon to be split open in readiness for picking. In another month, the roads would fill with machinery as another season reached an end. Once harvested, the farmer would plow under the rich soil for planting winter wheat or some other crop, and the cycle would continue.

When she reached the Big Muddy, she turned around and headed back for lunch. She was flying down the highway when a large shadow surrounded her bike. Cadin instinctively backed off the throttle and a crop duster shot ahead of her, the pilot waving as he banked and resumed the spraying of the cotton. She chuckled to herself and raced down the highway.

She found a parking spot in front of the diner and looked inside to see Emma and Serena busy serving customers. She sat on the bike watching as they bustled around the diner, as if they had worked together forever. Smiling, she removed her helmet and walked inside.

†

"Welcome back," Emma said as Cadin took a seat at the counter. "I take it you had a lovely ride?"

"Yes I did," she answered. "How did things go with you this morning?"

"Very well here too, I think we will make a good team."

"That's very good news. Did you tell her about the deal and the remodeling?"

"Yes I did, and she's excited to be working for tips. Would you mind if she went with us to Baton Rouge tomorrow?"

"The more the merrier," Cadin answered.

"Are you ready for some lunch?"

"I'll wait until it slows a bit and eat with you two if that's fine with you?"

"I'd like that," Emma said.

"I'm going to walk over to the park and make a phone call, but I'll be back for lunch."

†

Cadin found a bench under a tree and stretched out her long legs as she pulled out her phone and retrieved a business card from her wallet.

"This is Renee," a rich voice answered.

"Hi, it's Cadin. I hope I haven't caught you at a bad time."

"Not at all, I was just catching up on some notes. It's great to hear from you. Where are you?"

"Bogalusa, Louisiana," she answered.

"What on earth are you doing there?"

"It's a long story," Cadin said. "I'll tell you about it some other time. How have you been?"

Renee sighed. "Work has been crazy since I came back from the hunt, but it helps to stay busy."

Cadin sensed sadness in Renee's voice. "Is everything all right? You sound down."

Renee hesitated to answer.

"Renee, are you still there?"

"Yes, I'm sorry. I don't want this to sound desperate, but I wish you were close enough that we could get together this weekend."

Cadin felt a smile growing on her face. "That's not desperate, that's honest. I've been thinking about you this morning. I don't know exactly when I'm headed home, but I do know I'd like to see you again."

"I look forward to that," Renee said.

"The next few days are going to be really busy for me, but I'll give you a call this weekend if that's okay?"

"That will be perfect. Thanks for calling. It's good to hear your voice."

"I'll talk to you this weekend then. Goodbye, Renee."

"Goodbye, Cadin."

She slipped the phone back in her pocket and looked up at the clear blue sky. Things were falling into place here, and life was good in Greensboro. Content with the start she was able to make with the foundation, she decided it was time to start focusing on where she was going in her life.

Cadin entered the diner just as the last of the lunch crowd was leaving. "What's for lunch?"

"The special was bacon cheeseburgers and fries, but you can have whatever you want," Emma said.

"Boy, now that's an offer," Serena teased and Emma blushed.

"She's knows what I meant, you goof," Emma told Serena.

"The special is fine. What goodness did Merry come up with today?"

"The usual, and a chocolate silk pie I was hoping would last through the lunch crowd."

"Is that why you hid the last half in the kitchen?" Serena asked.

Emma shot her a glare and then smiled. "You don't have to tell everything."

"It must be really good pie. May I have a piece or are you coveting it for your own?" she teased Emma.

"No, smartass, I saved a piece for each of us, but if you two keep this up, I might just eat it all myself."

"You would too, wouldn't you?" Serena said.

"Danged straight, I would. Let's go get our lunch, and Cadin can pour some tea."

Serena followed Emma into the kitchen and she could hear them chatting away as they prepared their lunch plates. She smiled at how well the two were getting along, and knew they had made a good decision.

"Something smells good back there. What's for dinner?"

"Toni is making lasagna. We'll also have loaves of garlic bread and a fresh tossed salad."

157

"Count me in for dinner."

"Already have. Johnny will be here too. He called earlier to say he was coming to dinner."

"Are they still set to start the demolition in the morning?"

"Yes, and he's meeting the men from the shelter tonight to remove the tables and chairs."

"I think I'll grab a quick nap then," Cadin said as she was finishing off her portion of the pie.

Emma looked at Serena. "Do you need a break?"

"No, ma'am, I'm good. I would like to take a short break to visit that thrift shop across the street to pick up some clothes."

"There's no need for you to buy used clothes," Cadin said.

"I'm used to it. That's pretty much all I've ever had."

"Well, that's about to change. Forget the nap, we're going shopping."

Serena chuckled. "I did good on tips this morning, but not that good."

"Consider it a loan," Cadin said.

"There's no use arguing with her, you won't win," Emma added.

"Where is a good place to shop?"

"There is a small shop at the end of the strip that's good for blue jeans and tops."

"Is that okay to work in?" Serena asked.

"Yes, we keep it pretty casual here."

"Cool, let me get these dishes clean and I'll be ready to go."

"I'll get them. You two scoot," Emma said.

†

They found the shop easily in the small town and exited the store with six new pairs of jeans and a dozen shirts, new underwear, socks and two pairs of shoes. Cadin mounted the bike and then took the bags from Serena. "Let's drop these back at the hotel," she suggested as Serena climbed on the bike and took the bags.

Cadin pulled up in front of the hotel. "I'll wait here for you."

"I'll be right back then," Serena said and disappeared inside the hotel.

"Thanks for helping me get some new clothes," Serena said when she returned. "You're a good person, you know that?"

"Thanks, and you're welcome. All I ask is that you don't disappoint Emma. She's a good woman."

"She loves you too," Serena said, surprising her.

"What do you mean?"

"Her eyes light up and she smiles when she talks about you."

"That could just be gas," Cadin teased.

Serena laughed. "Face it, you can't take a compliment."

Cadin tossed up her hands. "You got me, but Emma and I have a special friendship. There's nothing romantic going on between us."

"Well whoever she is, I hope she realizes how lucky she is to have you," Serena said.

Cadin's smile faded. "She did. We were both lucky for a time."

"I'm sorry for opening my big mouth," Serena said, sensing she had touched a raw nerve.

"You couldn't have known about Missy," Cadin said.

159

"Will you tell me about her sometime?"

"No time like the present."

Cadin climbed from the bike and led Serena to a seat outside the hotel. Cadin took a deep breath and let it out slowly. It was getting easier to talk about Missy, but the pain of her absence still hurt.

"Missy was the best woman I could have ever dreamed of," she started.

Five minutes later, Serena was wiping tears from her eyes. She reached over and hugged Cadin. "I hope to find someone like that one day."

"You will, and when you do enjoy every minute you can together, because there are no guarantees in life."

"I will, I promise," Serena said.

"Let's get you back to work then if you're ready."

Serena wiped her eyes again and nodded. "I'm ready."

†

Cadin ate dinner with Johnny, then as the crowd started to thin out, they wiped down the tables and chairs. They carried them out onto the front sidewalk to make it quicker to load when the shelter truck arrived.

"There's no need to spend a lot of time on the floor in here tonight. It'll all be gone by tomorrow," he said. "I do need you to clear off the counter though," he told Emma. "We'll get that one out of here and install the new. Charles has already begun working on the new counter and is excited for you to see what he's come up with."

"I can't wait," Emma said.

"I hope by the time y'all return from Baton Rouge tomorrow night, you'll begin to see a huge difference."

"What do you hope to get done tomorrow?" Cadin asked.

"The first step is to get the counter, booths, and old flooring out. Once the flooring's removed, the painter will start on the walls. Another pair will be working on the bathrooms, and as soon as the crew arrives with the equipment, they will start removing the old and installing the new."

"What will take the longest?" Emma asked.

"The flooring is the most labor intensive, but we'll throw four guys at it, so it will go faster. We have to give the adhesive a night to dry before we can put any weight on it, so it will be critical to get it down tomorrow."

"Do you still think you will be done in three days?" Meagan asked.

Johnny grinned up at her. "You will be ready for a grand opening Monday as promised."

Cadin looked up the street and nodded. "Here's the truck."

It only took thirty minutes to load the tables with everyone helping. "What about those booths, what plans do you have for them?" the man from the shelter asked.

"We had planned to pitch them in the Dumpster. They would need major reupholstering," Johnny said.

"I have some men who would enjoy a project, and I have some fabric that was donated months ago that I need to get out of storage."

Johnny looked at Emma. She nodded and said, "Let's get to it then."

The dining room looked huge with the furniture removed. "It looks so much bigger when it's empty," Emma remarked.

"It will be all brand new and ready to go in no time," Johnny said as the truck pulled away. "I'll see you all late tomorrow then."

Emma turned to Cadin. "What time should we be ready to go?"

"Serena and I'll pick you up at seven, if that's not too early."

"That will be great," Emma said.

Cadin watched Emma and Meagan walk to their car and turned to Serena. "Are you ready to ride?"

"Yes, ma'am," she said.

†

When Cadin parked the bike at the hotel, Cadin looked at Serena. "Pack your bags and we'll load them in the rental car. When we get to your new home in the morning you can drop your stuff off then."

"That won't be hard to do," Serena answered. "Thanks again for everything," she said as they reached their rooms.

"You're welcome. I'll see you in the morning."

†

Cadin showered off and slipped into a hot soaking bath. The water soothed her tired muscles and as she relaxed her head against the wall, her thoughts drifted to the last few weeks of her life. With the help of her new friends, she was able to establish the first expenditures of the foundation's benefits in two small towns. Missy would be so proud of their accomplishments.

Cadin sank down to her neck in the water. Tears flowed down her cheeks as she thought of Missy and the upcoming anniversary of her death in a few short months. It was hard for Cadin to believe she had been gone for almost a year. She still found herself occasionally turning to say something to Missy, a wave of sadness filling her when she realized she would never be able to speak with her again.

When the water began to cool, Cadin wrapped her body in a thick towel and walked to the bedroom to get dressed for bed. She glanced at her cell phone and saw that she had missed a call. When she checked, she saw that Renee had called, but left no message. Cadin noted the time and thought it too late to call, but she would find time to give her a call tomorrow before it grew too late.

# Chapter Eight

At five, Cadin climbed out of the bed and showered. Memories of the past and questions about her future had made her toss and turn most of the night. As she stepped beneath the flow, she prayed the steamy water would help her shed the melancholy that threatened to ruin a happy day.

She picked up the keys for the rental car from the front desk and parked it in front of the hotel while she waited for Serena to arrive. She poured a cup of coffee that tasted like jet fuel and picked up the morning paper. Cadin was breezing through the sports section when the elevator pinged and Serena appeared pushing a luggage cart. She looked good dressed in some of her new clothes and wearing a huge smile.

"That is much better than the backpack you entered with," Cadin told her. "Do you need some help?"

"I think I can handle this."

Cadin tossed her the keys and walked to the coffeepot for a refill. The strong coffee sent a jolt of caffeine rushing through her as the funk that had clouded around her started to fade into the morning.

"Do you want to get some breakfast?"

"A cup of juice will work for now," Serena answered as she handed the keys back to Cadin.

"I'll be in the car," Cadin said.

Cadin lowered her sunglasses as she stepped outside the hotel and walked to the small SUV she had rented for the day. While she waited for Serena, she programmed the GPS to the address for the administration building on the LSU campus.

Serena slid into the passenger seat and looked at Cadin wearing a grin. "All set."

Cadin put the vehicle in gear and drove away from the hotel. "Have you ever considered college?"

"Not for me," Serena said. "I did good to make it out of high school."

"What are your plans for the rest of your life?"

"Right now, just surviving one day at a time," Serena answered with a frown.

"I think you are past that phase. You have a job, a roof over your head—"

"A new wardrobe," Serena cut in.

"So what do you like to do, or what do you want to learn to do better?"

Serena shifted in her seat.

Cadin sensed she was uncomfortable talking about her dreams. "If that's too personal, you don't have to answer."

"It's not that. I have loved drawing for years, but my mother always said I was wasting my time, but art is my passion."

"If you love it, then it's not a waste of time. Do you sketch, draw, or paint?"

"I have a sketchpad with pencil sketches. That's really all I could afford and carry in a backpack."

"Would you mind sharing it with me?"

More shifting in her seat followed her question. "I guess. It's not very good."

Cadin pulled the vehicle to a stop on the shoulder of the road.

"What? Right now?" she asked.

"No time like the present, besides we are early," she said. "Please?"

Serena stepped out of the car, walked to the back of the vehicle, and lifted the gate.

Cadin could hear her shuffling through the bags until she reached her backpack. The zipper opened and Serena stepped back to close the gate. She walked back to the door and slid into the seat. She hesitated for a moment before handing the sketchpad to Cadin.

She smiled and took the thick pad, resting it on the steering wheel and opened the cover. The first sketch threatened to take her breath away. A woman sitting on a timeworn couch looked wistfully out a window. The detail was amazing down to the fine crow's-feet on the woman's face. "This is beautiful. Who is this?"

"My grandmother," Serena answered. "She loved to sit and look out that window. She said she was watching birds, but I know differently. She was hoping someday her son would come home."

"Was he your father?"

"Yeah, he left for work one day when I was about five, and we never saw or heard from him again."

"I'm sorry to hear that. She's a beautiful woman."

"Yeah, she was. She died last year."

"You must miss her terribly."

"Yes, I do."

Cadin flipped the pages and became genuinely impressed with Serena's talent. "These are really good. Did you do some of these while you were on the road?" she asked as her eyes landed on a drawing of a crane similar to the one she had spotted a few days earlier.

"I was crossing a bridge a week or so ago when I saw him wading through a pond hunting frogs. He knew I was there, but stood rather impressively still as I sat on the bridge post and sketched him," she said with a smile on her face.

When Cadin looked up at her, she could see sparkling excitement in Serena's eyes as she told her about the bird. Cadin returned to the book and heard Serena gasp.

"What's wrong?"

"You're in there," Serena said.

"I am?"

"Yes, keep flipping."

Five pages further into the book, Cadin saw herself, sitting astride her motorcycle. The kid was good, as she managed every detail of the bike perfectly. "When did you do this?"

"I've been working on it for a few days. It's hard when you don't sit still for long," she answered.

"This is remarkable. I really like what you have drawn."

"Thank you," she said, a blush rising up her neck to color her cheeks.

"You have a great talent here. Have you ever painted?"

Serena's eyes dropped away from Cadin.

"I've never been able to afford the supplies. Maybe now that I'm working I can."

"Would you paint this for me?"

Serena's eyes flew back to Cadin. "You want me to paint this?"

"Yes, I believe that's what I just asked," she teased.

"I'd love to," Serena said.

"I'm sure we can find an art supply store in Baton Rouge." She handed the book back to Serena. "Thanks for sharing with me."

"You're welcome," she answered as she cradled the book against her chest.

†

When they pulled into the drive of a modest house, Serena looked at Cadin. "This is nice."

"Yes, it is. Come, I'll help you get unloaded."

Meagan raced out of the house when she heard the car door close and helped them carry Serena's belongings inside the house.

"Good morning," Emma said as the young women disappeared down a hall. "Would you like some coffee?"

"I'm good. I had two cups of the jet fuel the hotel serves."

Emma chuckled. "No telling how long it had been in the pot."

"Strong enough for at least a day or so," Cadin said, then smiled. "Are you two ready? We have one more stop to make while we're in Baton Rouge."

"Where else are we going?"

"We need to find an art supply store for painting supplies. I'm getting Serena to paint something for me. The kid has an amazing talent that needs some nurturing."

"Really?"

"Get her to show you her sketchbook sometime. She has a fantastic eye for detail."

"I will," Emma said as the two rushed into the room.

"All set?"

"Yes, we can get Serena settled in when we get back," Meagan said. "Let's rock and roll."

†

They sang along with the radio as Cadin drove. When they reached the Administration building, she handed Serena her cell phone. "Find us an art supply store, and then come join us. It shouldn't be hard to find us."

Serena smiled and began pushing buttons on Cadin's phone.

Cadin, Emma, and Meagan walked up the steps of the Administration building. A receptionist guided them to the Registrar's office and introduced them to Lucy Wills.

"Good morning," she said sweetly. "We have been waiting for your arrival. Your counselor sent your records to us yesterday, so we just need a few items to get you on your way to becoming our newest Tiger."

Meagan smiled brightly. "Sounds great."

Cadin left them to complete the application process while she went to the finance department to pay for the tuition. She was talking to the woman about books and other costs when Serena located her.

"Is this our newest student?" the woman asked.

"No, not me," Serena answered.

"Not yet, anyhow," Cadin said. "Did you find the store?"

"Yes, ma'am, I did. It doesn't look far from here."

"We can drop Meagan and Emma at Johnny's aunt's house and we'll go shopping."

"Awesome," Serena said. "Would you mind if I wait for you outside? It's such a pretty day."

"No, go ahead. I don't think we'll be much longer."

When she finished talking with the woman in finance, she had a better idea of what the additional costs would be for Meagan. She walked back to find them finishing up the application.

Ms. Wills smiled at Meagan when she handed her the completed application. "We will be sending you a packet this spring with your official admission letter and information about registering for classes and options for spending a week here for freshmen orientation."

"That sounds so exciting," Emma said.

"It will be a great time in your life," Ms. Wills told Meagan.

"I know I can't wait to get started." She hugged Cadin. "Thank you for making this possible."

Cadin hugged her back. "I did the easy part. You have four years of hard work ahead of you."

"I will make you both proud of me."

"I think I can speak for your mom and say we are already proud of you," she said.

"Most definitely," Emma said, placing her arm around her daughter's shoulders. "Let's go see where you'll be staying."

"Nice to meet you Ms. Wills," Meagan said.

"I look forward to seeing you again in a few months," she answered. "Stop in if there's anything I can help you with."

They left the office and started for the entrance. "Would you mind if I dropped you two off with Johnny's aunt while Serena and I do some shopping? Or better yet, you two drop us off and you can pick us up when you're done."

"That works for me," Emma said. "I'll treat us to some lunch then."

✝

Cadin opened the door to the art supply store for Serena then waved to Emma and Meagan before following her inside. Serena smiled as her eyes drifted to shelf after shelf of art supplies. Cadin went for a shopping cart.

"May I help you?" a young man asked when Cadin returned with the cart.

"We need all the basic painting supplies," Cadin said.

"Follow me then," he said and led them deeper into the store. "Watercolors, oils, or acrylics?"

"Acrylics," Serena answered.

He and Serena went to work, picking out supplies as Cadin wandered through the store. She picked out several sketchbooks, pencils, and charcoal for Serena to continue sketching. Cadin also picked out several instructional manuals on acrylic painting that Serena could use for reference. She placed the items in the cart as Serena was discussing the choice of easels and palette styles.

Cadin listened with interest as the salesman discussed various options with Serena and together they filled the cart with supplies, including a small adjustable folding stool she could set to whatever height was comfortable.

"There is one other item I would suggest purchasing if you don't already have one," he said, stopping in front of a display of tablets. "You can snap a photo of the subject you wish to paint and use it as a permanent resource. Very helpful if you are painting living beings, your subjects don't have to remain frozen modeling for hours."

"Set us up then with the best," Cadin said.

"These can get expensive," Serena said as she nearly drooled over the sleek devices.

"Would you be satisfied using cheap paints?"

"Probably not," Serena answered.

"Then don't settle for cheap equipment. Consider it an investment to improve your craft."

"I like the way you think," the young man said as he placed the tablet in the cart. "I think this will keep you busy for some time yet."

"Let's get settled up then," Cadin said and handed him a credit card.

Serena whistled when he rang up the total and looked at Cadin. "This is way too much," she said.

"Nonsense, you need all of the basic supplies to get started."

"It will take me forever to pay you back for this."

"Who said anything about paying me back? Consider it payment for the painting you have agreed to do for me."

Tears filled Serena's eyes as she nodded in agreement with Cadin's generous offer.

"Let's carry these bags out to the benches in front of the store while we wait for Emma and Meagan."

"Thanks for the business ladies," he said.

Cadin stretched her legs in front of her body as she relaxed on the bench, the sun warming her face. A cool breeze had begun to blow reminding her that the seasons were slowly changing.

"How much longer will you be staying in Bogalusa?"

"A few more days, until after the grand opening of the new diner," she answered.

"Where will you go from here?"

Cadin opened her eyes and smiled at Serena. "I'm going home."

"Will you be back?"

"I will, but I can't say when."

"Thank you for everything you have done for me, for us," she said as Emma pulled up to the curb.

"It has been my pleasure," she said as she stood and stretched. "Let's get this stuff loaded up."

†

Meagan told them about the house she would be living in when she started college. "Johnny's Aunt Sue is awesome. She's only going to charge me a hundred dollars a month if I help her with cleaning and cooking."

"That's a fantastic deal for both of you," Cadin agreed.

"It's a beautiful house and not far from campus at all," Emma said.

"Well, that brings us to another question. What will she do for transportation?"

"I have two good feet," Meagan said. "I can walk anywhere I need to go on campus."

"You will catch your death of pneumonia in the winter time," Cadin said. "I will take care of that, so don't worry about transportation."

"You have done so much already Cadin," Emma implored. "I will work something out."

Cadin didn't want to hurt Emma's feelings by insisting, so she decided to let it go.

✝

They finished their salads and Cadin looked up to Emma. "We're doing well on time. Do you want to see if we can find some artwork for the diner?"

"That's a good idea," Emma said. She paid the bill and they walked back out to the SUV.

They located a small studio and purchased several prints to decorate the walls then the four women drove back to Bogalusa.

"We got a lot done today. I hope the boys were as successful," Cadin said.

"We will see for ourselves in just a few minutes," Emma said.

✝

As Cadin rounded the last turn and pulled in front of the diner, the first thing she saw was the front window, *Missy's Place* was painted in an emerald green, a color reminding her of Missy's eyes. She felt her heart lodge in her throat, choking off her words.

Through the window they could see Johnny's crew working at a fevered pace. The walls were freshly painted, and men were laying floor tiles in three directions, having three quarters of the diner finished. She parked the SUV and they walked to the front door of the diner.

"Is it all right to come inside?" Emma asked Johnny.

"Yes, but can you come in from the back? The tile at the front door is freshly laid."

"No problem," Emma said and started to guide them around to the back entrance. She stopped when she realized Cadin wasn't following her. She looked back to find her studying the front window.

Cadin felt eyes on her and turned to see Emma smiling at her. "Go ahead, I'll catch up in a minute," she said.

✝

Emma stepped inside the back door and heard Meagan squealing in the kitchen. Emma walked inside to see her daughter running her fingers across the brand-new coffee machine that Meagan had requested. The kitchen sparkled with newness, the floors pressure cleaned, the areas needing grouting were complete, and shiny new equipment installed.

Emma's mouth was hanging open when Johnny walked up. "This is beautiful," she said.

"I thought you might like the way it turned out." He grinned.

✝

Cadin stood out front for several minutes, tears brimming in her eyes. "I hope you can see this, Missy," she spoke aloud. "The diner's coming along well. I know you would be proud."

Movement inside the building caught her attention. Cadin walked around the building and entered to find the others inspecting the newly remodeled and equipped kitchen.

"Wow, this looks great," she said.

"Wait until you see the bathrooms," Johnny said.

"Let's go look," Cadin told him.

The bathrooms were beautiful. The new floors, paint, and fixtures made the rooms brand new. "You put in new doors, baseboards, and crown molding too."

"I had some extras," he said.

"These look fantastic," she said. "How's the dining room coming?"

"Come, see for your own," he said.

Cadin followed him into the dining room as the men were finishing the last few sections of floor. When the final tile was ready to be placed, he looked to her. "Would you like to do the honors?"

"I think Emma should do that. Emma, can you come in here, please," she called out.

Emma, Serena, and Meagan filtered into the room. Everyone turned to look at her as Johnny held out the last square of tile.

"Would you like to do the honors?"

Emma nodded and turned to Meagan. "Will you help me?"

"Yes, Mama," Meagan said. They knelt down together and put the last tile in place.

"There," Emma said, her fingers tracing the edges of the tile.

The others clapped and cheered.

"Thank you all," Emma said as she stood and hugged Johnny and Cadin.

"What now?" Cadin asked Johnny.

"We let the floor settle tonight. Tomorrow we install the new counters, baseboards, and crown molding."

"We are planning a cookout for tomorrow night at my place. Would you and the crew care to join us?"

Johnny laughed. "You should know by now, we never pass up a free meal. What can we bring?"

"Healthy appetites," Emma said.

"That's never a problem. We're ready to clean up and lock the doors for tonight. Will we see you tomorrow?"

"Do you mind spectators?" Cadin asked.

"Absolutely not," he answered.

Cadin looked at Emma. "Why don't we watch until lunch and then head over to your place to prepare for dinner?"

"That sounds like a good plan."

"We will see you gentlemen tomorrow then," Cadin said and left with the other women.

They drove to Emma's and unloaded the art supplies and the prints they had purchased for the diner. As Meagan and Serena took the last load inside, Cadin turned to Emma.

"Can we cook steaks tomorrow?"

"Yes, that will be fine. I'll have to go shopping."

"Pick me up at the hotel early and I'll go with you. Think about what else we will be eating tomorrow night," Cadin said.

Emma nodded and followed the girls into the house.

†

It was still early when Cadin returned to the hotel, so she picked up her phone to call Renee.

"Hey," she said when Renee answered the phone. "Did I catch you at a good time?"

"Any time you call is a good time. Oh my goodness, that sounded cheesy didn't it?"

Cadin chuckled softly. "It's always good to talk with you too. How have you been?"

"Work has been so incredibly busy, but I'm doing all right. How is your trip going?"

Cadin spent the next several minutes telling her about the diner remodel, then Meagan and Serena. "That's such a beautiful story. You're a great person to give these women such a positive future. Missy would be proud of the things you have already accomplished."

"I think she would too. I've been doing a great deal of soul searching on this trip as well and I think I know where I'm heading once again."

"I'm glad it's been a therapeutic time for you. I hope you're heading home soon."

"I will be. I think the time away from the city and getting out into the fresh air has helped to clear all the confusion I've been experiencing over Missy's death."

Renee remained silent for several long seconds as Cadin paused. "I'm glad to hear you're headed back this way. I'm excited at the prospect of seeing you soon."

"I am too. It's time for me to start moving on with my life and stop dwelling on the past. The last thing Missy would want is for me to struggle like this."

"You've been through a great deal in the last year," Renee reminded her. "You needed this time to find you."

"I have to admit something to you, Renee."

"I'm listening."

"I'm strongly attracted to you, but I'm in no means done grieving my loss of Missy. I don't want you to feel like you're being compared to a past life that can never be replaced."

"I can understand your hesitance to start new, and I'm a very patient person. I'm attracted to you too, and would like to get to know you better." She paused briefly. "And if nothing more than a friendship develops then I'll be content with knowing I have a great friend. I have to be honest with you too though. I want more than that with you. I think together we can build a future that is good for both of us."

"I'm so excited about getting to know you," Cadin said.

"So you get your cute butt home soon," she teased.

Cadin chuckled at her comment. "It won't be long now."

They talked for a while longer and when the call ended, Cadin felt a wave of relief wash over her. Since meeting Renee, she had felt a chemistry between them. She was relieved to hear that Renee was interested in building a life together. She knew it wasn't going to be easy, letting go of Missy, but in her heart she knew it was the right move to make.

She slept, a deep peaceful sleep, until the alarm jarred her awake.

# Chapter Nine

Cadin and Emma left the market with beautiful steaks, corn, other fresh vegetables to cook, and ingredients for a fresh salad. "Let's drop these at home and go see what the boys are up to," Emma said.

They carried the groceries inside and Cadin saw the prints sitting in the living room. "Let's take these and get the boys to hang them for us."

"Great idea," Emma agreed.

Cadin carried them out to the car. "What are the girls up to this morning?"

"Getting Serena all settled into her new home," Emma said.

"Do they want to go to the diner with us?"

"No, they said they would make the salad, and get the other vegetables ready while we're gone."

"Okay, will you drop me off to get my bike?"

"Sure thing," Emma said and slid in behind the wheel.

†

Cadin settled onto her bike and fastened her helmet before starting the motor. The familiar vibrations between her legs felt good, and she couldn't hold back a smile at the thought she had just had. It was the first remotely sexual thought she had experienced in months. She grinned, kicked the bike in gear and rode to the diner.

Emma was unloading the prints as she pulled up beside her and parked. "Can I help with those?"

"I've got them if you'll just get the door," she answered.

Cadin held the door open and one of Johnny's men rushed over to take the prints from her.

"Let me get those for you, Emma," he said and smiled sweetly.

"Thanks, Bobby," she said as she relented to his assistance.

Cadin whistled loudly. "This place is looking great."

Johnny looked down from nailing a section of crown molding and smiled. "Good morning, ladies."

One of the crew entered carrying a new table, another followed with two chairs, and they placed them in the middle of the room. "Now you can have a seat, ladies," he said.

"These turned out very nicely," Cadin said as she sat in one of the seats. "Very comfortable too," she added.

"We are assembling the rest of them now while they finish the baseboards and molding," the man said.

Johnny climbed down from the ladder. "You are just in time," he said.

"Just in time for what?" she asked.

"To see your new counter being installed," Johnny said as he pointed toward the kitchen.

Two of his men were rolling a huge counter carefully across the new floor. "We're going to need everyone's help to move this thing," Charles said.

"This turned out beautiful, Charles," Emma said as she walked over and ran her hand along the smooth edges.

"It was a pleasure to make for you, Emma. I've eaten many a good meal at the old one and hope to eat many more on this one," he said.

"Starting with breakfast Monday morning," Emma said.

They watched as the men lifted the counter off the dolly in two large sections and bolted it to the floor.

By the time the counter was finished, it was time for Emma and Cadin to head back to Emma's to begin working on dinner.

†

Cadin pulled out the grill from the garage and prepared the charcoal for lighting. When she entered the house, Emma and Meagan were busy in the kitchen rinsing the chopped vegetables for cooking. The potatoes were in the oven baking and Serena was preparing pitchers of tea.

"Do you think we should sauté some onions and mushrooms for the steaks?" Emma asked.

"I think that would be a lovely touch," Cadin answered. "Is that bread I smell baking?"

"Yes, Serena and I were digging through the freezer and we found several loaves, so we thought we would bake them," Meagan said.

"Great idea," Cadin said as she swiped a section of carrot and bit into it. "Have you turned the steaks?" she asked Emma.

"Nope, I left that for you."

Cadin walked to the refrigerator and pulled out a large pan holding the steaks, placing it on the counter. She used tongs to flip the steaks, dredging them through the marinade mixture. "I can't wait to sink my teeth into one of these," she said as she covered them and returned them to the refrigerator.

"What can I do?" Serena asked.

"You can slice those mushrooms and I'll slice the onions," Emma said.

"I can do them both," Serena said.

"Have at it then." Emma grinned.

"What about me, Mama?" Meagan asked.

"You and Cadin can set up the spare tables and chairs in the backyard."

Cadin followed Meagan to the garage and they carried out two folding banquet tables and a dozen chairs, setting them up on the patio. The men would be arriving within the hour, so Cadin lit the fire to prepare the coals for cooking, then followed Meagan back inside.

No sooner had she stepped into the kitchen than her phone rang. She looked at the display to see that Lexie was calling her and stepped back outside to take the call.

"Hello, Lexie."

"Hi, Cadin, I got the phone today."

"So I see. How are you?"

Lexie rattled on excitedly about starting school, her new friends, and how much fun she was having in school for almost ten minutes, barely pausing to take a breath. When she stopped talking, she regrouped and asked, "When are you coming back?"

"Soon, I think," she answered.

Lexie pried for more detail. "As in next week?"

"Possibly, but I don't know for sure yet."

"Oh I hope so, Cadin, I have so much to tell you."

Cadin chuckled. "I will see you as soon as I can, and that's a promise."

"Goody," Lexie giggled. "Mommy's calling me to dinner. I love you."

"I love you too, see you soon."

"Hurry," Lexie said. "Bye for now."

"Goodbye," she said and tucked the phone back in her pocket.

The back door opened and Serena came out carrying the container of steaks. "Are we ready to start cooking? Johnny called and they are on their way."

"I guess we'd better get cooking then," Cadin said.

†

The dinner turned out wonderful and when the crew left to return home, Johnny lagged behind.

"We will finish the last touches on the diner tomorrow, and I have Hank from the Health Department scheduled for eight on Monday to certify the new facilities. If all goes well, you will be open for lunch."

"After the inspection, I'd like you and the boys to enjoy the first unofficial breakfast, on the house, since I did promise Charles," Emma said.

"We would love that," Johnny said.

"If you will prepare the final bill for tomorrow, I'll bring you a check," Cadin said.

"I will," Johnny said and bid them all a good night.

Cadin finished carrying the tables and chairs back into the garage. "I think I'll head out too. I'm in desperate need of a shower."

"You did an excellent job on the steaks," Meagan said.

"Thanks."

"I'll walk out with you," Emma said.

They walked to Cadin's bike and then Emma grabbed her up in a hug. "Thank you again for everything. You've made my dreams come true and Meagan is so excited about college, she can barely wait until the fall."

"You know she could take some courses online, once she's accepted."

"I'll have to get her a laptop then," Emma said. "She's going to need one for college anyhow."

"May I do that as an early graduation present?" Cadin said.

"I feel bad. You've done so much for us already."

"Please, I'd really like to do this for her."

Emma nodded her consent. "Thanks."

"My pleasure," Cadin said and mounted the bike. "See you tomorrow at the diner?"

"Yes, that will be great. I want to work on some new menus and get acquainted with the new equipment."

"See you then."

✝

Cadin woke early the next morning and rode south until she found a store with an electronics department. When she exited, she carried a laptop bag full of equipment from a top-of-the-line laptop, headphones, jump drives, and a compact portable printer. She strapped the bag onto the bike and returned to Bogalusa by midmorning.

She parked and walked into the diner. Squeals were coming from the kitchen, so she placed the computer bag on the floor and stepped inside to see what they were all the excited about. Serena, Emma, and Meagan were staring at a commercial waffle iron, watching the timer tick down the final seconds.

"I don't remember a waffle iron on our list," she said, startling them.

"Johnny got this for us," Meagan said. "Isn't it wonderful?"

"Smells great," she answered.

"Have a seat at the counter and you can be our first guinea pig," Emma teased. "I'll bring you a waffle and some fresh coffee out in a minute."

"Would you mind if I steal Meagan?"

"No, go ahead."

"What did I do now?" Meagan asked, but followed Cadin into the diner.

"Nothing, I wanted to give you an early graduation present," Cadin said as she picked up the computer bag and handed it to Meagan.

"What's this?"

"It's a laptop, silly. You will need one for college, and if you're interested, you can use it to take some online courses this spring to get a start on college. But first, I thought you could design a new menu for your mom."

Meagan was speechless for several long seconds, until the reality of the moment struck home. "Oh my God, Cadin, thank you," she said and grabbed her in a hug.

"You're very welcome," Cadin said. "It probably needs charging, so why don't you plug it in?"

Serena and Emma were smiling as they watched through the serving window.

Meagan carefully placed the bag on the counter and opened it, taking out the laptop and charger. "This is beautiful," she said as she plugged the cord into the computer and opened the lid.

"Incoming," Emma announced as she walked into the room carrying a plate with a golden brown waffle.

"That came out perfect," Cadin said as Emma placed it in front of her. "You know, chicken and waffles is all the rage right now in Atlanta and other places. Do you think Bogalusa is ready for that?"

"I think that will be the first new item on our menu," Emma said.

"Why don't you try them out on the crew tomorrow morning? If they pass their approval, I think they would be a success."

"That's a great idea. I'll need to make a run for some chicken tenders today."

Cadin poured syrup over the waffle and cut the first bite as Serena carried out another plate.

"Here you go, boss. Yours is cooking, Meagan."

"Thanks," Meagan answered, barely looking up from the laptop.

Cadin moaned as she took a bite. "This is really good. I'd be surprised if they aren't a best seller."

"Relatively easy to prepare too," Emma said and took a bite. "These are good."

"There are so many ingredients you can add too," Cadin said, "to give the customers a variety to choose from."

"Like what?" Meagan asked as she took up a pen and made ready to take notes.

"Let's see. Chocolate chips, pecans, blueberries, strawberries, peanut butter chips, for starters," Cadin said. "I'm sure we could think of other items."

"Dried cranberries," Serena said.

"Diced fruit like apples and peaches," Emma said.

"See, it's only limited by your imagination." Cadin grinned.

†

They were deep in the development of a new menu when Johnny and several of his crew arrived to put the finishing touches to the diner.

"Good afternoon, ladies," he said.

"Hey Johnny, how are you today?" Emma asked.

"I couldn't be any better," he answered with a smile. "If you'll tell me where you want those prints hung, we'll do them for you."

"You have a deal," Emma said.

Emma and Johnny experimented with placements. Meagan and Serena were busy working on the new menu. Cadin smiled as she watched them work and then let her eyes take in the redesigned diner. *My work is complete here.*

"I'm going to head out unless you need me for something," she told Emma.

"No, I think we've got it from here," Emma answered. "Will you come over to the house later for some dinner? Meagan and Serena are making spaghetti tonight."

"That sounds great, what time?"

"Six okay with you?"

"That will be perfect."

†

Cadin left the diner with a specific destination in mind. An hour later, she pulled up to Rupe's and carried a six-pack of Abita beer into the office. Rupe was on the phone when she entered and smiled when he looked up to see who had arrived.

"Welcome back, Cadin."

"I thought I'd take you up on your offer of lunch if it still stands."

He smiled when he saw what she was carrying. "Excellent! Let's get those brews on ice and go get some fresh mudbugs."

Rupe placed the beer into a small cooler and filled it with ice. "These will be perfect when we get back."

Cadin followed him out to the dock and climbed aboard the airboat. The afternoon was gorgeous as they rode through the bayou to check his traps. The first one they came to was full of the tiny lobster-like creatures.

"Bingo," he said with a smile as he emptied the trap in his bucket. "These will make for some good eating."

They returned to the dock and carried the bucket back to the office. "I've got a cooker out back. I'll get it started if you want to grab us a beer. Are you going to be able to drink and ride that bike?"

"I'll have one with you while you cook and then the food will soak it up."

"I have some sodas in the fridge for your meal then."

"Perfect," Cadin said and walked inside for the beers.

Rupe started the gas burner and had added water to a large pot he set on the fire. "We'll let this get to boiling and then I'll put the bugs on."

"Is there anything I can do?"

"You can go inside and bring out this morning's paper and spread it out on the table. Do you like hot sauce for dipping or some drawn butter?"

"Hot sauce will do just fine."

"There's a new bottle in the fridge and you'll find bowls in the cabinet above the sink."

Cadin returned inside for the supplies and smiled as she heard Rupe whistling as he worked.

† 

When the mudbugs had finished boiling, Rupe lifted the basket onto the side of the pot to let the water drain, then poured the contents onto the newspaper-covered table. "If I knew you were coming I could have gotten some corn and taters to add to the boil," he apologized.

"This is perfect as it is," she answered.

They let the steamy pile cool for a few moments while Cadin returned to the kitchen for a soda, a fresh beer for Rupe, and a roll of paper towels. When Rupe picked up a mudbug, Cadin watched as he separated the head from the body, sucked the juices from it, and dropped it to the paper and began to peel the tender meat from the body. He smiled up at her. "No worries, you don't have to suck the heads," he chuckled.

"That's a relief," Cadin said with a smile as she dove into the pile of food.

"Enjoy yourself, little lady," he said.

"You're absolutely right, Rupe. These are better fresh out of the water," Cadin said as she peeled another mudbug and dipped it in hot sauce.

The old man smiled, very pleased his guest was enjoying the impromptu meal. "The only way they should be eaten."

Enjoy it, she did. They ate in silence for a while before Rupe looked up at her. "You're leaving soon aren't you?"

"Yes I am, probably tomorrow," she answered.

"I hope you will journey back this way again."

"You can bet on that," Cadin said as she dipped another morsel. "If, for nothing else, but to share a lunch with you," she said.

Rupe chuckled. "You sure know how to make an old man's day."

She smiled back at him. "You can cook for me anytime."

After they finished off the meal, Rupe wrapped up the shells and carried them to a compost pile.

"I hate to eat and run, but I need to get back to town."

"No problem, thanks for coming back to have lunch with me."

"I'm so glad I did. I'll never forget this meal," she said.

"Hurry back for another then," he said and offered his arms for a hug.

Cadin accepted his hug. "Just keep an ear open for me," she said.

"You be careful on that thing," he said, nodding toward the bike. "Watch out for gators," he reminded her.

"I will," Cadin said, then mounted the bike and rode back to the hotel.

✝

She checked the time after she emerged from the shower and saw that the day had slipped quickly away from her. She dressed and rode to Emma's for a final dinner together.

Serena and Meagan had done an excellent job with the spaghetti dinner. There was salad left over from the night before and a loaf of bread they toasted with garlic butter.

"This is fantastic," Cadin said.

"Glad you like it," Meagan said.

During the meal, Cadin told them about her lunch with Rupe and they talked about the menu and the reopening of the diner.

"I'm so excited, I may not be able to sleep tonight," Emma said as they girls cleared the table.

"It has turned out beautiful, hasn't it?"

"I couldn't be more pleased."

"I think Johnny fudged on the final bill a bit. It wasn't nearly close to his original number."

"Lower?" Emma asked.

"By about ten thousand," Cadin said.

"I will make sure he doesn't pay for a meal for a long time to make it up," she answered.

Cadin smiled. "I think that's a perfect solution."

"Will you join us for breakfast in the morning?"

"I'd love too. What time?"

Emma cocked her head to think for a moment. "Hank will be there at eight to do the inspection, and he works pretty quickly. How about eight forty-five?"

"I'll be looking forward to chicken and waffles," Cadin said. "If you ladies don't need my help, I think I'll head back to the hotel and see you in the morning."

"We've got everything under control here," Meagan said. "Thanks again for the laptop."

"You're welcome," Cadin said.

"May I walk out with you?" Serena asked.

"Sure," Cadin said.

"What's up?" she asked Serena, after bidding Emma and Meagan goodnight.

"I just wanted to thank you for everything. I think you saved me from making a horrible mistake. I also wanted to tell you I've started your painting."

"Awesome," Cadin answered. "I look forward to seeing the finished product."

"I hope you'll be pleased."

"I'm sure I will be."

"Goodnight Cadin," Serena said and hugged her tightly.

"Goodnight," she answered and when Serena released her, mounted her bike for the ride back to town.

✝

Cadin pulled her duffel from the closet and began packing her belongings. A sense of sadness threatened to overwhelm her until she thought of all the good things that had happened to her on this journey. The people she had met and was able to assist in improving their lives would live in her heart forever.

She left out fresh clothes for the ride then slipped into the bed, exhausted from the long day.

†

Cadin walked into the diner the next morning to find Meagan busy at work behind the counter. "What are you doing here? I thought you'd be in school."

"Teacher workday," Meagan said. "I'd forgotten about it until I arrived at school today, so I'm hanging with Mom, helping her with the grand reopening."

Cadin's eyes followed Meagan's as they drifted toward the duffel strapped on her bike. "Tell me you weren't going to skip town without saying goodbye?"

"No, I wouldn't do that. I planned to fake my way into the school as a relative to say goodbye."

"No need to fake, you are family," Meagan said.

Cadin took in her words, a warmth spreading through her. She knew Meagan would not have said that without sincerity. "I hope the inspection is over. I'm starving."

"Have a seat and I'll bring you some coffee. Mom's just finishing up with Hank now."

Cadin sat next to Charles at the counter. "You did a wonderful job on this counter."

"Thanks, it was a challenge, but one I thoroughly enjoyed. I plan on making this my spot for a long time." He grinned.

Emma entered the dining room and escorted Hank to the door with Johnny in tow. As soon as Hank left the building she turned and held up the copy of his inspection report. "Our first one hundred percent," she said and walked behind the counter to hang it in the new frame. "Everyone ready for some chicken and waffles?" she asked.

"Heck yes," came the chorus of responses.

"Let's get to cooking, ladies," Emma said as Johnny took a seat beside Cadin.

"I'm glad everything passed with flying colors," she told him.

"Me too," he said. "I never doubted it for a minute, though. Emma, on the other hand, has been pacing the new floors since seven."

"She should be very proud of the new diner. You and the crew did an excellent job."

"You made it possible," he reminded her. "Without your influence and financial assistance, Emma would have been forced to close within the year."

"This should keep her going for a long time."

"Yes, it should. I told her I'd be glad to help her out with any repairs she may have, even after the warranty runs out."

"You're a good man, Johnny," Cadin said as she slapped him on the shoulder, "A good friend too."

Johnny glanced out at her bike. "You're leaving today, aren't you?"

"Yes, it's time for me to go home."

"I wish you would reconsider and decide to call this place home."

"It is home for me in a way, but it's time for me to move on with my life."

Cadin swore she saw a tear in Johnny's eye when he said, "We're all going to miss you."

"I'll miss you too, but I'll be back to check on things from time to time."

"That's good to know," he said as Emma walked behind the counter carrying the first two orders of chicken and waffles, placing them in front of Cadin and Johnny.

"If it weren't for you two, we wouldn't be here celebrating today. I hope you enjoy."

"Thanks," they said in unison.

"Let's do this," Johnny said as he poured syrup over his waffles and handed Cadin the dispenser. "How do we eat this anyhow?"

"Just like this," Cadin said as she cut a bite of chicken tender, then a bite of waffle, which she speared, and then speared the chicken tender. She lifted the fork to him in demonstration and placed the food in her mouth.

The crew burst out laughing and watched as Johnny took his first bite. His eyes grew wide and he moaned his pleasure. "This is really good," he said after swallowing. "I was worried about the combination, but I now see what all the fuss is about."

Emma's smile grew wide as she accepted his praise.

"Good job, ladies," Cadin said. "I've never eaten better."

†

Once the crew had finished eating and left, Emma and the girls shared a late breakfast.

"That duffel on your bike says you're leaving today," Emma said.

Cadin smiled warmly to her new friends. "It's time for me to go home."

"We're going to miss having you around."

"I've enjoyed spending time with you all. I will be back to visit."

"I hope you will at least come to my graduation," Meagan said.

"I wouldn't miss it. Do you still have my business card?" she asked Emma.

Emma nodded. "Yes, I do."

"I'll be expecting an invitation from you in a few months then," she said.

Serena shuffled in her seat. "How will I get your painting to you when it's done?"

"You can have it shipped to the address on the card. I'll reimburse the cost of shipping to you."

"You've got to be kidding," Serena said. "After all you've done for me, for us, there's no way you're paying for shipping."

"It won't be cheap," she warned.

"I'll have tips saved up by then," Serena said.

Cadin nodded her head. "Very well then." She stood to leave.

"You're leaving now?" Emma cried.

Cadin looked at her new friend. "I've a long ride ahead of me, and you three have a reopening to prepare for," she said.

"Will you call and let me know when you've made it home?" Emma asked.

"It will be a day or two yet. I've got a stop to make in Alabama."

"That's fine. Please don't forget to send me a picture of Missy for the front wall too."

Cadin's eyes flew to the sign painted on the front window and smiled. "I will make it my first task when I get home."

Cadin hugged each of them and then walked to her bike. She looked at the signage one last time, waved to the three women standing in the doorway, and kicked her bike into gear.

She raced north for several hours, before stopping to refuel and stretch her legs. The late afternoon sun made the leaves on the trees glow in shades of brilliant gold and orange as the seasons were about to shift. Summer had somehow slipped away on her journey. She rode for another hour before reaching the sign announcing the Greensboro city limits. Minutes later she pulled into Sister Frances's drive. She had only been gone a little over a week, but it already felt like a homecoming to her. She rang the doorbell and waited patiently for the door to open.

Sister Frances opened the door and gasped when she saw Cadin standing there. "Cadin, it's so good to see you," she said as she held the door open. "Come inside."

"Thanks. I was hoping I could spend a night or two here again. I'm on my way home, but promised Lexie, I would come by to visit."

"She will be so excited to see you and of course you can stay here. Why don't you drop your bag in the sleeping quarters and ride over to Miss Betty's house. You're welcome to dinner here, but I doubt Lexie will let you leave so quickly."

"You're probably right. How have you been?"

"Busy, but good, the work keeps me going. I'll have you know we sold all of the pecans on our first weekend at the market."

"That was a lot of nuts." Cadin chuckled.

"Yes, it was. I didn't think we would ever finish shelling them. That was the most harvested in many years."

"Any changes around here?" she asked.

"Another woman showed up and stayed a few days on her way to family. She was beaten badly, nearly broke, so we did our best to patch her up and send her on her way with a full tank of gas and hopefully enough money to make it to Enid."

"That's good. I'm glad she escaped that environment."

"Me too," Sister Frances said.

"I'll drop my bag and see you for coffee in the morning," she said. "Thanks."

"You're very welcome. Enjoy your visit."

Cadin placed her bag on an empty bed and rode her bike to Miss Betty's house.

✝

Nothing could mask the sound of the bike's motor, so as she pulled into the drive at Miss Betty's house the door flew open and Lexie came rushing outside.

"Cadin," she yelled. "It's really you."

"Yes, it is," she said as she bent down and picked up the small girl in her arms and twirled her around. "I think you missed me."

"I did, and I'm so glad you're back even if it is just for a day or two."

When she placed Lexie back on the ground, the little girl took her hand and led her inside the house. Terri and Miss Betty were busy in the kitchen.

"Welcome back, stranger," Terri said. "Have you eaten yet?"

"Nope, I was hoping you'd have enough for one more."

"Of course we do. Welcome back, Cadin," Miss Betty said. "Are you staying with us tonight?"

"I've already dropped my bag at Sister's," she said. "She told me I could have my old bed for a couple days."

"I'm so glad you're here," Lexie said as she led her to the kitchen.

"So how have you all been?"

"I've been promoted to assistant manager at work," Terri said.

"That's great news," Cadin said as she hugged Terri then took Miss Betty in her arms. "And you, lovely lady? What have you been up to?"

"Just getting settled back in my home," she answered. "I've been doing a bit of gardening too," she smiled. "It's too late to get anything in the ground until spring, but the ground will be ready when it warms up in the spring."

Terri handed her a platter of pork chops. "Put these on the table and we'll bring the rest in just a minute. Lexie will you pour the tea?"

"Yes, ma'am," she answered and poured three glasses of tea. "We need one more setting." She turned to find Miss Betty holding another glass of ice.

"I'll bring you a plate and some silver," Miss Betty said.

"Is there anything I can help with?"

"No, we've got it under control."

Lexie walked around the table and handed her a glass of tea.

"I swear you have grown an inch or two. What have you been feeding this child?"

"She's had plenty of protein and fresh vegetables," Miss Betty said. "I've never seen a child attack field peas like Lexie does. It does my heart good to see her eat so well."

"Let us also warn you about her love for Miss Betty's corn bread. If you want a piece, get it when it first arrives. She loves it too."

"Yes, I do," Lexie, answered with a giggle.

After dinner, they moved to the living room to be more comfortable and Cadin told them about her time in Bogalusa. Lexie sat so close to her she was almost in her lap.

"You have been a busy woman since you left us," Miss Betty said.

"So much has happened so fast, my head spins sometimes," she admitted.

"You've done good things for so many people," Terri said. "Most will never experience in a lifetime what you've done in a matter of weeks."

"It's a good start, and now I think I know where I want the foundation to go, so it's time to go home."

"I hope you'll take some time off for you before rushing back to work," Miss Betty said.

"A few days yes, but I'm eager to get back to work."

"It will be there waiting for you when you return."

"How well I know." She grinned.

Cadin noticed Lexie's eyes getting heavy and realized it was later than she thought. "What time do you get out of school tomorrow?"

"I'll be home by three," she said.

"I'm going to head out to get some rest and so you can go to bed to be fresh for school. If it's okay with Miss Betty, I'll come back tomorrow."

"You are welcome at any time."

"Is there anything I can help you with?"

"You can run the tiller for me in the garden if you must get your hands dirty," she teased.

"Sounds like a plan." She hugged them all goodnight.

†

As promised, she shared coffee and breakfast with Sister Frances. "I'm going to do some tilling for Miss Betty today. Is there anything I can do for you while I'm here?"

"No, Cadin, you've done enough, but thank you for helping Miss Betty. Will I see you tomorrow?"

"You bet. I can't leave without one of your breakfasts to send me on my way."

"I will send you off with a full belly then," Sister Frances said.

†

When she arrived at Miss Betty's, the woman was already working in the garden.

"I have her all gassed up and ready to go," Miss Betty said when she saw Cadin.

"I'll get to it then," Cadin said and cranked the tiller. By lunchtime, she had the entire garden spot turned and mulched for the winter.

"If you don't mind, put the tiller back in the shed and come in for a sandwich."

"Thanks, and then if you don't mind I'm going to go back and clean up before Lexie and Terri come home. What plans do you have for dinner?"

"I've got a pot of chicken and dumplings cooking and planned to bake some fresh biscuits. Is there something in particular you wanted?"

"I was going to invite you all to dinner, but I won't pass up your home cooking."

Miss Betty chuckled. "Ham and cheese okay for lunch?"

"Perfect," Cadin answered. "I'll be there in just a few minutes."

†

Cadin was sitting in the swing when the bus pulled up to drop Lexie home from school. She rushed up to her and sat in the swing beside her. "Did you have a good day in school?"

"Yes, ma'am, I kicked in the winning run in kickball today too," she said.

"That's awesome! You know what I'd like to see?" Cadin asked her.

"What?"

"Show me what pictures you've taken on your camera."

Lexie raced inside the house and returned with her camera. She climbed back into the swing and handed Cadin the camera. Miss Betty followed her out of the house carrying a small tray.

"I thought you two might care for a snack," she said as she placed the tray on the swing beside Lexie. "Let me know if you need anything else."

"Thanks, Miss Betty," Lexie said sweetly.

They ate the snack and then Cadin scrolled through the pictures Lexie had taken as she described each one to her.

Terri pulled up from work, just as they were finishing. "Hey, you two," she said.

"Welcome home, Mommy," Lexie said and rushed over to kiss her. "Did you have a good day?"

"I did. How about you? How was your day?"

"It was great. I kicked home the winning run in our game."

"I'm so proud of you, honey."

Terri looked at Cadin. "How was your day?"

"Good, I got the garden tilled and ready for winter. I have a feeling I'm going to be a bit sore tomorrow though, but it felt good at the time."

"I hear Miss Betty has chicken and dumplings on the stove for dinner."

"Word does travel fast in small towns," Cadin teased.

"It does, but, actually, this time Miss Betty told me before I left for work today," Terri said with a chuckle.

"I see," Cadin said with a grin.

"Do you two mind if I join you? It's so pretty outside today."

"No, not at all," Cadin answered.

"I'll go change clothes and take that tray back if you're done with it. I'll check on Miss Betty too, while I'm in there."

They watched as Terri walked inside and then resumed swinging. "She's right you know. It's a beautiful day. It'll turn cold soon and I bet we get snow this year."

"I've never seen snow," Lexie said.

"It's cold and wet, but beautiful all at the same time. A lot of fun to play in too, but you have to be dressed warmly."

Terri walked back outside and joined them on the swing. "Mom, Cadin says we're going to get snow this year."

"That will be fun. I hope it comes on my day off, so we can play in it," Terri said. "It's nice to see the changing of the seasons. There is nothing but a sea of green in Florida. The gold and oranges of the leaves is a nice change."

"It's a lot warmer in Florida though."

"That's true. We'll have to go coat shopping for you soon," Terri told Lexie.

They enjoyed the warm sun of the autumn afternoon until Miss Betty called them in for dinner. Lexie raced ahead to wash her hands. "Do you really have to leave so soon?"

"Yes, I don't want to get stuck riding in the wet and cool weather. It's coming soon. I can feel it in my bones. I didn't bring my leathers to keep me warm when I ride.

"I can understand that, but I still hate to see you go."

"I'll be back," she said as she held the door open for Terri.

When Cadin left that night, she hugged Lexie tightly. "I won't see you tomorrow before you leave for school, so tonight's goodbye for now. You have the phone now, so call me when you want."

"I will call you every weekend," Lexie said as she began to tear up.

"Be strong for your mommy and Miss Betty. Help out when you can."

"I will," she said between sniffles. "I love you."

"I love you too, Lexie. Sweet dreams tonight."

"Go ahead and brush your teeth while I walk Cadin out," Terri told her.

"Hurry back to us, Cadin," Miss Betty said with a hug.

"I'll be back before you know it," she answered.

Terri held the door open and they walked out to her bike. "I wonder if I can ask one other favor of you?" she said.

"Anything I can do," Cadin answered.

"I want to ask you to be Lexie's godmother in case anything happened to me. Mind you, I don't plan on going anywhere, but it doesn't hurt to plan. I know how much she loves you, and I know you would give her the moon if you could."

Cadin felt a lump form in her throat. What she was asking was a complete surprise. "I would be honored," she answered. "What do you need me to do?"

"Would you draw up papers to give you guardianship of Lexie, if anything happened to me? I'll get them notarized or whatever I need to do on this end."

"Yes, that is a simple request."

"Thank you, Cadin."

"You're welcome," Cadin said and hugged her. "Take care and I'll send those papers soon, so relax."

"Goodnight. See you soon," Terri said and turned to walk into the house.

Cadin pulled the bike onto the road and saw a small shadow in a bedroom window. She knew that Lexie was watching her leave. *Wow, a godmother, no one's ever asked me that before.*

# Chapter Ten

With a stomach filled with bacon, eggs, and toast, Cadin mounted her bike and left Greensboro for the second time. This time, though, she was heading home. For the first time in several months, the word home sounded good to her ears. Far too long after Missy's death the home they built together had felt like an emotional prison for her, painful memories of Missy stalking every room, every corner of the apartment.

Eager to return, she felt confident that the time she had spent on her journey had made her strong enough to co-exist with the memories of Missy, and understand that nothing or no one could ever replace the love they had shared. Would she love again? Possibly, but it would be an entirely different love than the one they shared.

✝

Cadin's luck held out and she reached her building before rush hour traffic had snarled every street in town. She parked the bike in her assigned spot and removed her duffel, then covered the bike to protect it until she again felt the need to have the wind in her face. Shouldering the bag, she walked to the elevator and rode it to her floor as thunder rumbled in the distance. In addition to beating the rush hour traffic, it appeared she also escaped an approaching thunderstorm.

She unlocked the door, carried her bag into the bedroom, and dropped it on the floor. The first thing she wanted to do was take a long, soaking bath. The exertion of using the garden tiller and the long ride home left her body aching and exhausted. She turned the water on for the bath and stripped out of her riding clothes. Pouring scented bubble bath into the water, she reached for a bath pillow, and stepped into the hot water, sinking up to her neck in the silky bubbles.

The warm water relaxed her muscles while the scent of the bubbles soothed her mind, Cadin soaked until the water turned cool and her skin began to prune. She released the trap and stepped from the tub, drying with a large towel before wrapping her body in a plush robe. She poured a glass of wine and walked to the glassed-in balcony as the storm raged in full force. Taking a sip of wine, Cadin felt her hand lift and touch the glass, tracing the path of a raindrop as it streaked down the glass like a tear and fell to the earth, many floors below. "Like the thousands of tears I have cried for you, Missy," she spoke into the silence of the apartment.

✝

During the next two months, Cadin shipped a framed photograph of Missy to Emma, and forwarded the guardianship papers to Terri. The Missy Foundation flourished and she, Missy's sister, Marilyn, and her law partner, Pam, waded through hundreds of applications for assistance, to find those that called to their hearts.

She and Renee also started down the path of a new relationship. Her first weekend home, she spent touring the city with Renee, showing her all the places she loved. They spent several hours sitting in her favorite park, enjoying a beautiful late fall day. She told Renee about her life with Missy.

"I can't imagine losing anyone that way, especially my partner."

"It has been, by far, the worst experience I have endured in my life. For a long time I wasn't sure I would survive the heartache. When my business partner suggested I take a sabbatical to find myself again, it was the best thing that I could have done."

"So that's how you made it to Greensboro?"

"Yeah, I put a map on the wall, threw a dart and it landed on Greensboro."

"Are you serious? That's how you ended up there?"

"Yes, it is. It worked out well, so when I finished what I needed to do there, I pulled the map out again, and that's how I ended up in Bogalusa."

"You really did put yourself in fate's hands."

"The people I encountered on my journey made me realize I have so much more left to do, and how much love I have to give."

"I hope I can help with that," Renee said, a blush rising to her cheeks.

"You are," she answered.

†

Cadin cooked them a delicious meal and they sat for hours on the balcony talking, getting to know each other as they finished off a bottle of wine.

At one point, Renee looked at her, smiling and her lips begging for a kiss. Cadin felt her body lean forward and then stop.

"I hope you don't find me boring."

"Not at all," Renee answered. "I understand that you've been through a very traumatic period during the last year."

"I'm very interested in you, but—" she said.

"But you need to finish mourning for Missy. I understand that, and I will wait as long as it takes."

"Thank you for understanding and being patient."

"If you haven't already figured it out Cadin, you are a very special person. I knew that from the first time we met at the hunt, and I haven't been able to stop thinking about you."

Cadin leaned down and kissed her softly on the lips. "I hope I won't disappoint you."

"I doubt that you could," Renee answered.

†

When they decided it was time to retire for the evening, they walked into the apartment. Renee had placed her bag in the guest room, planning to sleep there. She turned to walk into the room and Cadin took her hand to stop her.

"Will you stay with me tonight?"

"Of course, just let me get ready for bed."

Cadin dressed in shorts and a T-shirt then climbed into bed to wait for Renee.

When Renee entered the room, Cadin pulled back the covers and waited for her to climb into the bed. "Would you mind if we spooned tonight?"

"Not at all," she answered with a smile as she turned onto her side.

Cadin wrapped her body around Renee's and draped her arm across her waist. Renee reached to take her hand, entwining their fingers.

At first, Cadin felt tense lying so close to Renee, but her body slowly relaxed as she buried her face in Renee's hair and breathed in her scent. A smile played across her face as she closed her eyes and slept peacefully wrapped in Renee's warmth.

✝

During the next month, they spent every weekend together. Cadin realized how much she enjoyed spending time with Renee and felt her heart opening to her.

When Renee invited her to spend the weekend with her in Stone Mountain, Cadin was ready to take the relationship to the next level.

✝

Renee had soft music playing on the stereo during the meal and after they finished eating, Cadin held out her hand.

"Dance with me."

"I'd love to," she said, taking her hand.

Cadin took Renee in her arms. She could feel Renee's body trembling as they moved fluidly together around the small room, her face buried in Renee's neck. Her lips couldn't resist the temptation of kissing her neck. When her lips continued their exploration, she found they had sought out Renee's lips and they kissed, softly at first. As the kissed deepened, Cadin felt her body responding and allowed her hands to explore Renee's body.

Renee's moan vibrated in her mouth as their tongues danced sensually. When Cadin broke the kiss to look into Renee's eyes, she found them sparkling with excitement.

"Are we ready for this?"

Renee answered by taking her hand and leading her into the bedroom.

†

Renee's soft lips kissed her awake the next morning.

"Wow, that was incredible," Cadin said as she stretched on the bed.

"You were definitely not a disappointment," Renee said as her tongue swirled around an aroused nipple.

Cadin's soft moans echoed through the room as her hand filled with Renee's hair and she pulled her mouth down to cover her breast. "I hope you don't have plans to leave this room today," Cadin said with a grin.

"Not a one," Renee answered as she kicked the covers off the bed.

†

On the anniversary of Missy's death, she received two items. First, the painting from Serena had arrived at the office during the early morning. She had captured the spirit of Cadin's journey in the painting. She cleared a wall in her office to hang it there. The second arrived by courier just after lunch. Cadin looked at the outer envelope for several minutes before opening. The bastard didn't have the courage to face her and deliver it himself, but he did deliver it as ordered. She opened the envelope and removed the check for one hundred thousand dollars.

She let the check drop onto her desk. "It will never be enough, but it is a start," she said and walked out of the office.

## Epilogue

Each year in August, Cadin and Renee took two weeks off to attend the annual dove hunt, and to visit Bogalusa. The dove hunt was as festive as ever and each year they celebrated for those who had passed on to a different journey. Terri and Lexie never moved out of Miss Betty's home. They had become such a tight-knit family there was no sense in renting or buying another house. The rent money, saved as startup money was now a college fund, even though Cadin knew in her heart that her goddaughter would not pay a cent toward a college education.

Lexie was blowing through elementary school and well on her way to junior high. She had grown nearly as tall as Cadin on Miss Betty's home cooking and was turning into a beautiful young woman. Terri was now the manager of the grocery store after her former boss retired, and Sister Frances still opened her home and her heart to women in need. Her age was creeping up on her and she relied more on Miss Betty and Lexie for help, but she refused to close the shelter.

The trips to Greensboro were highlighted not only by the annual dove hunt but also the harvesting of the pecans, which had brought Cadin and Lexie so close together. It was a tradition they would continue for many years.

Meagan graduated with honors from LSU and began teaching second grade in Bogalusa. The day of her graduation was a very proud moment for Cadin. Without the benefit of the foundation the world would have missed out on a beautiful teacher. The second year she taught, Cadin sat in on her classroom for a day and wasn't surprised at how much the students adored their teacher. Meagan had found her calling.

The diner was still a thriving business and a landmark in Bogalusa. Emma and Johnny had fallen in love and they were married on Cadin's third trip back. It was a beautiful event and she was so happy it made Cadin's heart smile.

Serena never made it to LSU, but found her love in painting. She still works with Emma at the diner in the mornings then spends the rest of the day painting in her studio. Several times a year she would show and sell her work in a prominent gallery in New Orleans and her art became widely popular with the elite society. They hadn't admitted it yet, but Cadin felt that she and Meagan had fallen in love. They shared a home together on the outskirts of town and Cadin suspected they were not open in their relationship due to Meagan's teaching position. Some things took more time to change, but they were still young and in love.

Speaking of being in love, Cadin and Renee have built a life together, and celebrate many happy adventures. They anxiously await the legalization of same-sex marriage so they can celebrate their love with their extended family and friends. Renee surprised Cadin last Christmas with a ring and a positive pregnancy test.

Their child would be born at the end of June. Just in time to travel to her first dove hunt.

The End

# About the Author

## Ali Spooner

Ali Spooner is a native of Florida, currently living and working in Memphis, TN. Home for Ali is Pensacola, Florida where she has a partner of twenty years, one son and a grandchild that has her wrapped completely around her little finger. Her other children are all four-legged, three dogs and two cats, and her dearest companion in Memphis, Rascal, a rescued tiger kitten named after her favorite country group.

A true daughter of the South, Ali enjoys spinning stories about the South, the strong, but gentle women and creatures that make it a wondrous place to live.

As an "Indie" author, Ali has been writing for many years as a hobby. After a cancer diagnosis in 2010, she decided to take a leap and start self-publishing and has published over a dozen stories. Ali's characters range from cowgirls and psychics, to a healthy dose of supernatural beings. She has written stand-alone titles and series. Ali frequently writes several stories at a time, depending on which characters are bouncing around loudest in her head.

Ali is an avid reader and her other hobbies include photography, outdoor activities, and watching college sports.

# Other Books from Affinity eBook Press

**Once Upon a Time—Alane Hotchkin** Many centuries ago, a vision came to the royal seer with a prophecy that showed a warlord ruling the land until she came to claim what was rightfully hers. Princess Kataryna's widowed father, King Theos, raised her from birth, to one day, become queen and rule over Pavlone. When she turned fifteen the princess had no idea that the Fates would start her on an obscure path to her final destiny. On that day as she rode into a meadow of wildflowers a dark rider came upon her, thus beginning her tumultuous journey of love and adventure. Raven only wanted to escape the blows that life had dealt her. She longed to be on the open sea and free. When she came upon a beautiful young girl sitting alone in the middle of a meadow, little did she know that her destiny would be changed forever. Will they become the pawns of the ancient vision or will both paths lead to the same port of destiny? Find out it in this exciting high seas adventure that will capture your imagination.

**Asset Management—Annette Mori** Toni, Sophie, and Kim, are the modern day version of Robin Hood blended with the Three Musketeers. For the past eighteen months, they have been moving the assets of the rapacious bank executives to the more deserving coffers—at least in their minds—of the poor and middle class. When a mysterious woman keeps crossing paths with Toni, sparks fly. Is it a coincidence or all part of some greater master plan? Is she friend or foe? Add the Russian mob, the FBI, and an all-female covert organization and you have the perfect recipe for danger, intrigue, and even love. Does the trio join forces with *the organization*? Follow the twists and turns to the explosive conclusion. Not everything is black and white. There are many shades of gray and sometimes it's difficult to decipher who is good and who is evil. No one is all virtue or all malevolence, but sometimes love helps us rise above.

**Do Dreams Come True?—JM Dragon** Laurel Rogers was unceremoniously dumped by her long-time lover, painter Ronnie Lancaster, finding her belongings outside the apartment they shared. To add to her misery, the next day she loses her job, fired by the Dragon of Finance, Christen Jamison. What else can go wrong? Oh yes, her best friend becomes engaged to the brother of the Dragon. For ten years, Christen Jamison has never forgiven her partner for walking out on her. She's given up on love, making her work her life as the accountant for the family business. After she is directed to fire a woman who should never have been on the redundancy list—Laurel Rogers—Christen begins to doubt her commitment to the store's management and policies. How do two people who really shouldn't get on end up in a relationship? Find out in this deliciously ordinary romance.

**Return to Me—Erin O'Reilly** Renowned microbiologist Sydney Tanner left work as normal for her trip home but never arrived. Ellie Scott her wife of ten years frantically, to the point of obsession, attempts to find her—the only evidence there is something amiss is Syd's crashed truck, then the clues go cold. Ellie refuses to believe that she will never see Syd again but realizes many months later with nothing solid to go on, it's time to attempt to move forward with a life without Syd. Leaving her hometown she accepts a new job at Salvation, aptly named for Ellie's predicament. There Ellie meets beautiful Maya Rojas who is the director of Salvation—a rehabilitation hospital. Although she hasn't given up on finding Syd, Ellie finds herself increasingly drawn to Maya. Will Salvation bring just that to Ellie, allowing her to find peace and happiness again, or will it have her questioning all that she believes in? A wonderful romance cloaked within an intriguing mystery.

**Terminal Event—Ali Spooner**  Tally Rainwater was born with the gift of second sight, something she never understood. A near-fatal accident, at age twelve, makes her visions clearer, but not the reason for them. As she matures, Lisa, a spirit, enters her visions to guide her in using her gift, but still not the reason why. After Tally's gift helps locate the body of a murdered teen, she realizes her gift is to help lost souls find their peace. When it's discovered, a serial killer murdered the teen, Blair "Spooky" Cooper is the Agent in Charge assigned to the case. A task force of local detectives and FBI forms to track the killer. Blair enlists the aid of Tally, and together with the team, Tally helps them piece together the puzzle of murders spanning twenty years throughout the Deep South. Even with the complication of the case, Blair and Tally have an undeniable attraction to each other. As they close in on the killer, the killer focuses on Tally, jeopardizing her bond with Blair and everyone around her. For the sake of the case, they put their attraction on the back burner until the killer is caught. Will the killer be caught or continue to evade authorities? Can Tally and Blair's budding romance survive the possibility? Read this intense murder mystery romance and find out.

**Arc Over Time—Jen Silver** Dr Kathryn Moss has job offers flowing in after her exciting archaeological discoveries at Starling Hill the previous year. Now she has choices to make that could jeopardise her relationship with Denise Sullivan, the fiery journalist, who has become her lover. For Denise the choice seems obvious. She thinks they have moved beyond the casual sex stage to something more like a true relationship. However, she's not sure how to handle Kathryn's continuing infatuation with Ellie Winters. Ellie's new career as a promising artist proves to be a catalyst for the simmering tensions in relations between her wife Robin, Kathryn, and Denise. Will Denise persevere in her pursuit of the reluctant professor? Does Ellie have anything to fear from Kathryn's fascination with her art, or is there another motive behind the professor's obsessive interest? This wonderful romantic continuation with the characters from *Starting Over* ties up loose ends. But the question is—does everyone have a happy ending? A must read.

**Presence—Charlene Neal** After catching her husband red-handed in bed with his secretary, Kayleigh Gibbs takes her daughter and her Jeep and flees across the country. She opens up her own veterinarian practice, and they move into an old, secluded farmhouse in Hoekwil, South Africa. At her best friend's housewarming party Kayleigh meets the beautiful and enchanting Rebecca Steward. Rebecca is instantly drawn to Kayleigh, but is still recovering from a breakup—her girlfriend left her for a man. She's afraid of a repeat performance with Kayleigh, and won't pursue a romantic relationship with her, preferring instead to develop a platonic friendship. When odd, inexplicable things start happening on the farmhouse, a terrified Kayleigh turns to Rebecca for comfort, only to find herself developing unexplainable feelings for her new friend. Rebecca, despite her best intentions, is falling in love with Kayleigh. But when Rebecca moves in with Kayleigh to help her get to the bottom of the haunting, she finds more than she bargained for. Can Rebecca and Kayleigh overcome ghosts from the past and their own insecurities, or will a presence from the past tear them apart?

**A Walk Away—Lacey Schmidt** Kat and Rand's daily worlds are 2,100 miles apart, but something about their meeting on the magical shores of the nation's oldest national park east of the Mississippi sparks questions that neither woman can just walk away without answering. Sometimes chance brings you to the right person to help you resolve some of your baggage, and you learn to like yourself a little more. Kat and Rand are smart enough to recognize this chance in each other, but they also find that there is a catch to every opportunity—walking toward something is always walking away from something else.

**Love Forever, Live Forever—Annette Mori** No one forgets their first love. For Nicky, that's Sara, who abruptly disappears one day, leaving only a cryptic letter. That day scarred her soul. When the pain starts to diminish, Nicky begins to get her life back on track until it is derailed once again by an unimaginable twist. Changed forever, Nicky becomes a careless, womanizing nomad known as the Little Wild One, until she meets Annie. Thirteen years later,

Nicky's finally settled and happy. Fate intervenes and puts her directly back into the path of her first love, Sara, and the corresponding events send her into a tailspin. Now she must decide—who will be the person she ends up living with and loving forever?

**Possessing Morgan—Erica Lawson** New York City, in the height of summer. Crime seems to have taken a holiday, and Detective Morgan O'Callaghan is bored, bored, bored. Paperwork is mating and multiplying on her desk, and even a jaywalker is starting to look good. Anything to get her out from behind her desk! Enter Andrea Worthington, Charleston socialite and all-around rich girl, right down to the wealthy fiancé. She's also the new Assistant District Attorney assigned to Morgan's precinct. Their first meeting is like two freight trains crashing head-on. Then a high-profile, career make-or-break murder case throws them together again. The investigation has barely begun when Andrea becomes the target of a nearly fatal hit-and-run. But was it really aimed at her? Can she and Morgan find the common ground they need to solve the case and stop the attacks, or are the gaps just too wide to bridge?

**Twenty-three Miles—Renee MacKenzie** Talia Lisher has a long family history of lying, about anything and everything. With her father dead, and her mom gone on a quest to start a new life, Talia struggles to keep in touch with her only remaining family, her incarcerated brother. When Talia sets her sights on Officer Shay Eliot, she vows to stop lying. She starts watching Shay, waiting for just the right circumstances and amount of courage to talk to her. Talia might be watching Shay, but someone in a dark van is watching Talia. Is the mystery driver a dangerous part of her family's past, or is it all just a coincidence? Shay Eliot has left the police force because of what she perceives as a hostile work environment. When a brutal double-murder on the 23-mile-long Colonial Parkway puts the FBI's magnifying glass squarely on her, her alibi comes from an unlikely source—a young woman who has been stalking her. Shay wants to keep her distance from Talia, but once she gets to know the younger woman she can't keep feelings from developing. This is a story about community, and how it comes together in dangerous and devastating times. When you don't know who to trust, you better have friends who will rally around you. Will Talia and Shay find the answers they need to the mystery of the murders on the parkway, or will justice be elusive? Will they survive their quest for the truth?

**Confined Spaces—Renee MacKenzie**  Andie Waters spends her days pulling waste samples for environmental testing and at night, she tends bar at The Cave, a popular hangout for straights in a small Georgia town. Serial monogamy has grown stale for her, so she's content working to pay off her debts and hanging out with her old hound dog. Or so she thinks, until a beautiful lesbian drops by The Cave. Andie suspects her involvement with the woman will be only temporary. Little does she know no part of her life will be left untouched. Kara Travis likewise anticipates nothing more than a brief fling upon meeting Andie, especially given her reputation as both a personal ice princess and a corporate hatchet wielder for Royal Environmental. What luck to find a hot lesbian bartender in nowhere rural Georgia. Andie and Kara spend a passionate weekend together and find that their notions of no strings attached are far from accurate. Their supposed short-term ideal diversion of a commitment-free romp hits a major complication when they come face-to-face with one another at Royal Environmental's offices Monday morning. While carrying out her duties, Kara discovers crimes being committed by and against Royal Environmental employees. Will Kara be forced to shut down the Georgia Division of the company? If she does, Andie will lose her job. Worse yet, Kara may lose Andie before she's really even sure she's got her. Corporate politics, complicated romance, and long distances conspire to keep Andie and Kara all boxed in. Can love triumph despite the Confined Spaces?

**Reece's Star—TJ Vertigo** Reece Corbett watches over the dancers in her gentleman's club with the blue, razor-sharp eyes of The Animal. Few know that resting comfortably in her office is her newest love, a tiny MinPin named Smudge. What happened to The Animal, known for her rapacious appetite for women and danger? Faith Ashford is what happened to The Animal. Faith and Reece have been together a while now and they have settled into something resembling domestic bliss. This bliss alarms Reece. It's one thing for Faith to see her softer side, that's vulnerability enough, but to let her friends see it…no. Not the best plan. Under Faith's guiding, loving hand, will Reece successfully traverse the rocky road of emotion and embrace the positive changes in her life? Or will she panic and be unable to control that Animal part of herself? Will she take that next step to declare herself fully capable of love and devotion? This third installment in the popular series that began with *Private Dancer* continues the passionate and often hilarious romance of Reece and Faith as they both grow in love and in trust.

**Flight—Renee Mackenzie** It's 1983 and Kate Hunter is a student at a small, private college in Virginia. When Lana coaxes her onto the back of her beat-up scooter one night, Kate's education starts to encompass more than just her pre-vet studies. Kate has always done as expected of her, so when she starts staying away from home on weekends to spend time with her new lover it's way out of character for her. Lana is secretive, but Kate accepts things as they are and gives Lana her space. When she feels the sting of betrayal, will she be able to continue giving Lana her privacy? Kate's sister April is a high school student playing with fire as she parties with her older boyfriend, Boyd. After finding someone overdosed the morning after a big party, April grows weary of all the drugs and alcohol. Will she be able to convince Boyd that they should slow down? Will she be able to pull it together before it's too late? Kate and April are forced to face up to events from their younger years, their mother's desertion, and their long-deteriorating relationship with one another. Some lives will be lost and others changed forever when the sisters' lives intersect. Will they be consumed by the wreckage, or will they be able to pick themselves up and take flight?

**Reflected Passion—Erica Lawson** Where passion, reality, and destiny combine. Dale Wincott is a 27-year-old woman born into Bostonian wealth and groomed to marry into the social hierarchy. Her mother is a hard-hearted society matriarch, but her father feels for his daughter and helps Dale find a life on her own as a furniture restorer. Françoise Marie Aurélie de Villerey is a 28-year-old Countess, born into the French aristocracy and forced to marry a count much older than herself. For ten years, she was his trophy wife, forced to endure his perverted desires, until the day he finally died. He had broken her emotionally and she no longer cared for what life had to offer, slipping from one sexual partner to another as often as she changed her clothes. Until... that one night when Françoise looked up during a sexual encounter and saw Dale watching her from the mirror. A veritable angel, full of innocence and curiosity, who touched her very soul. Through the mirror, Françoise embraces life anew, while for Dale it is a powerful awakening, forcing her to discover not only her sensual nature, but the inner strength she possesses.

**The One—JM Dragon**  Phil (Philomena) Casters loves her work as a pilot, above everything else in her life except Ming, her married lover. Phil needs to enhance her status in the community before asking Ming to leave behind her wealthy husband. Rosa Moran is a teacher, raised by missionaries in China after the death of her parents. She loves the country of her birth and the people. Her English grandfather desperately wants her to live with him to atone for the guilt he feels about the death of her parents. He sends her a letter requesting her to come home. When Phil flies to the mission to deliver the letter to Rosa, neither can envisage the chain of events about to take place. It starts as a collaboration to save four children, leading them to the surreal private paradise of Langshow. Could this be the perfect place for the children and Rosa to settle? Phil is not so sure. Chang, an old friend from Rosa's childhood lives in Langshow and makes no bones about the fact that he wants Rosa. All thoughts of Ming disappear as Phil tries to fight her attraction to Rosa. However there is the little matter of an innocent misunderstanding—Rosa thinks Phil is a man. *The One* is a romance with everything, love, intrigue, misunderstandings with a happy conclusion—the only question—who gets the girl?

E-Books, Print, Free e-books

Visit our website for more publications available online.

www.affinityebooks.com

Published by Affinity E-Book Press NZ LTD
Canterbury, New Zealand

Registered Company 2517228

Made in the USA
Coppell, TX
15 January 2021